"So The Life Of A Pampered Princess Isn't All It's Cracked Up To Be, Is It?"

Jacob asked, cocking his head.

"I won't make excuses for who I am, or how I was raised," Clair said defensively. "Or who I thought I was, anyway."

He'd been around spoiled, wealthy women... but there was something different about Clair, an innocence that unnerved him. He swore softly and scooped her up in his arms. She gasped, then stiffened at his unexpected maneuver.

"Since you don't want to miss out on anything, I suggest we get you into bed."

Her eyes widened. "I never said, I mean, I certainly wasn't implying that I wanted to, I mean, that we should—"

He carried her to the bed. "Relax, Clair. I meant to sleep. We've got a long couple of days ahead of us." He dropped her on the squeaky mattress. "But thanks for thinking of me."

Her cheeks turned scarlet against her pale skin. She looked so lost lying on the bed, so...disappointed, that Jacob considered joining her.

This, he thought miserably, was going to be one long trip....

Dear Reader,

Revel in the month with a special day devoted to *L-O-V-E* by enjoying six passionate, powerful and provocative romances from Silhouette Desire.

Learn the secret of the Barone family's Valentine's Day curse, in *Sleeping Beauty's Billionaire* (#1489) by Caroline Cross, the second of twelve titles in the continuity series DYNASTIES: THE BARONES—the saga of an elite clan, caught in a web of danger, deceit...and desire.

In *Kiss Me, Cowboy!* (#1490) by Maureen Child, a delicious baker feeds the desire of a marriage-wary rancher. And passion flares when a detective and a socialite undertake a cross-country quest, in *That Blackhawk Bride* (#1491), the most recent installment of Barbara McCauley's popular SECRETS! miniseries.

A no-nonsense vet captures the attention of a royal bent on seduction, in *Charming the Prince* (#1492), the newest "fiery tale" by Laura Wright. In Meagan McKinney's latest MATCHED IN MONTANA title, *Plain Jane & the Hotshot* (#1493), a shy music teacher and a daredevil fireman make perfect harmony. And a California businessman finds himself longing for his girl Friday every day of the week, in *At the Tycoon's Command* (#1494) by Shawna Delacorte.

Celebrate Valentine's Day by reading all six of the steamy new love stories from Silhouette Desire this month.

Enjoy!

Joan Marlow Golan

Joan Marlow Golan
Senior Editor, Silhouette Desire

Please address questions and book requests to:
Silhouette Reader Service
U.S.: 3010 Walden Ave., P.O. Box 1325, Buffalo, NY 14269
Canadian: P.O. Box 609, Fort Erie, Ont. L2A 5X3

That Blackhawk Bride

BARBARA McCAULEY

Published by Silhouette Books
America's Publisher of Contemporary Romance

 SILHOUETTE BOOKS

ISBN 0-373-76491-X

THAT BLACKHAWK BRIDE

Books by Barbara McCauley

BARBARA McCAULEY,

who has written more than twenty novels for Silhouette Books, lives in Southern California with her own handsome hero husband, Frank, who makes it easy to believe in and write about the magic of romance. Barbara's stories have won and been nominated for numerous awards, including the prestigious RITA® Award from the Romance Writers of America, Best Desire of the Year from *Romantic Times* and Best Short Contemporary from the National Readers' Choice Awards.

One

"Clair, for heaven's sake! How will Evelyn ever get this done if you don't stop fidgeting?" Josephine Dupre-Beauchamp glanced at the gold Rolex watch on her slender wrist, sighed, then frowned impatiently at her daughter. "Now stand up straight, dear, and goodness, keep your chin up. The wedding is only three days away and this has to be *perfect*."

Josephine, with her willowy figure and stunning dark looks, was herself a picture of perfection. Some said that her daughter looked just like her, though Clair was three inches taller and her eyes were blue instead of Josephine's brown. "From our French ancestors," Josephine had always proclaimed when anyone commented on her daughter's striking eye color.

While Josephine circled, Clair sucked in her stomach, gritted her teeth against the pins sticking in her bust and waist, then rolled her shoulders back and lifted her chin.

She couldn't breathe, couldn't move, and an annoying, persistent itch stabbed the center of her back. *Three days.*

As if Clair needed her mother, or anyone else for that matter, telling her that her own wedding was only three days away.

To be precise: seventy-eight hours, forty-two minutes and—she looked up at the wall clock in the exclusive bridal shop fitting room—thirty-seven seconds.

Clair swallowed the lump in her throat. From the triple mirrors in front of her, three identical young women dressed in white satin and Italian lace stared back. It was odd, Clair thought, that the reflecting images didn't really look like her at all.

Didn't *feel* like her.

"She's lost weight." Evelyn Goodmyer, the hottest and most sought after couturier in all of South Carolina, pinched the seam under Clair's arm and frowned. "She was a perfect size six when we measured four weeks ago and her bust was a 34B. How can I possibly—"

"Ohmigod, Jo-Jo!" Victoria Hollingsworth burst into the fitting room, waving a newspaper. "Wait until you see *this!*"

Momentarily distracted by the triple reflection of herself in the mirrors, Victoria tucked a short red curl behind her ear, then smoothed a hand over her ecru raw silk trousers.

"*Vickie.*" Josephine crossed her arms and arched an impatient brow.

Victoria dragged her gaze from the mirror, then

snapped open the newspaper and thrust it under Josephine's nose. "This morning's *Charleston Times*," she said, smiling brightly. "Society section, center page."

Victoria had not only been Josephine's college roommate at Vassar University, she was also Clair's godmother. And—Clair felt her heart skip as she glanced at the clock again—in seventy-eight hours, thirty-nine minutes and twenty-six seconds, Victoria would become her mother-in-law, as well.

Clair craned her head slightly to get a view of the paper, but could only see the picture of a charging bull running amuck in a china shop on the back page.

Victoria quickly snatched the newspaper back and started to read, "'Oliver Hollingsworth and his fiancée, Clair Beauchamp, photographed while attending a charity ball last week in support of the new children's wing at St. Evastine's Memorial Hospital, will wed this Saturday at Chilton Cathedral.'"

Josephine brushed an imaginary piece of lint from her beige linen jacket. "That's it?"

"Of course not, silly." Victoria cleared her throat. "'Ms. Beauchamp, twenty-five, daughter of shipping magnate, Charles Beauchamp III and Josephine Dupre-Beauchamp, longtime residents of Rolling Estates in Hillgrove, is a summa cum laude graduate from Radcliffe University. Oliver, twenty-six, son of Nevin and Victoria Hollingsworth, also residents of Rolling Estates, recently received his M.B.A. from Harvard after graduating Phi Beta Kappa from Princeton. He is currently manager of accounts at Hollingsworth and Associates accounting firm in nearby Blossomville.'"

Victoria's eyes filled with tears and her voice wavered. "My little boy's all grown up, Jo-Jo. And Clair, our beautiful, precious Clair—"

Both Victoria and Josephine looked at Clair and sighed.

Stop! she wanted to yell at them. Stop, stop, *stop!* Between her mother and godmother these past few weeks, Clair had seen more female tears than a boy band concert.

When Evelyn jammed another pin into the pearled bodice of the wedding dress and hit skin, Clair felt her own eyes tear.

"Shame on you, Vickie, you're making her cry, too." Sniffing, Josephine took the newspaper from Victoria and folded it. "You can read this later, Clair. We've got to hurry if we're going to make our eleven thirty lunch reservations at Season's."

Clair opened her mouth, but before she could speak, Evelyn cut her off.

"I can't possibly finish that quickly," the couturier insisted. "And she still needs to try on the shoes you've ordered. She can meet you there when we're done here."

"I suppose that will be all right." Josephine stepped close to her daughter and pressed a kiss to her cheek. "I'll send Thomas back to pick you up, dear. Call me when you're on your way and I'll order for you."

While Evelyn walked Josephine and Victoria to the front of the shop, Clair turned back to the mirrors and stared.

This time, the tears that burned her eyes had noth-

ing at all to do with sharp pins. She looked at the
clock again.

Seventy-eight hours, twenty-nine minutes and
twelve seconds....

Jacob Carver was in a hell of a bad mood. He supposed the ninety-degree heat and one hundred percent
humidity inside his car might be the reason. Or perhaps it was because he'd driven twelve hours straight
through from New Jersey last night and hadn't seen
a bed in twenty-four hours. Or quite possibly his foul
disposition had something to do with the fact he'd
been sitting across the street from this fancy bridal
store for two hours, sweating his butt off, without so
much as a glimpse of the woman.

What the *hell* could she possibly be doing in there
for two hours?

Not that he really wanted to know, Jacob thought
as he reached for another bottle of water from the
foam ice chest on the front seat of his car. There were
areas where he preferred to maintain his ignorance.
Anything connected to weddings was at the top of the
list and a female shopping was a close second. The
less he knew about those things, the better.

He guzzled half the bottle of water, then tossed it
back in the cooler. The upside was that the mother had
left a half hour ago with another woman. Since he'd
had explicit instructions from Lucas Blackhawk that he
was to approach Clair Beauchamp only if she were
alone, Jacob figured his window of opportunity would
be opening any minute now. Based on the tight leash
the Beauchamps kept on their only daughter, Jacob also
figured he might not get another opportunity.

And Lord knew, if Mommy and Daddy Beauchamp
caught sight of a long-haired private investigator

speaking to their precious little girl, they'd probably call the cops and have him locked up faster than he could say Jack Daniels. It wouldn't matter that he hadn't broken any laws, either. The rich had their own set of rules, their own laws.

And he had his.

But he had no intention of going to jail. Not for anyone, or any amount of money. He'd do what he'd been paid to do, then he'd hit the road again. Because he specialized in the most difficult, or most touchy, location of missing persons, his referral work took him all over the country. It kept him on the road more than at his apartment in New Jersey, but that was fine with him. Jacob liked to keep moving, and he liked to move fast.

And he had the car to do it in—a '68 Charger 426 Hemi, stroked and bored to 487 cubic inches. Restored meticulously by his own hands, his baby was all muscle and speed. On the open road, she could do a quarter-mile in 10.6.

He just might see if he could break that record after this job was done. Maybe he'd head down to Miami for a couple of weeks, find a warm, sandy spot on a beach and share a pitcher of margaritas with...what was that waitress's name he'd met last year when he'd been staking out a con artist at a resort hotel? Sandy—that was it. Blonde and buxom and happily divorced. He smiled at the memory, realized he'd been working too many hours for way too long. All work and no play had indeed made Jacob a very dull boy.

But all that was about to change.

Jacob sat abruptly when the woman came out of the bridal shop. She carried a shopping bag in one hand and a small clutch purse in the other. The sun shimmered off her baby-blue silk tailored pantsuit and picked up the strands of red in her shoulder-length dark hair. He watched as she slipped on a pair of sunglasses, then stood in front of the shop, glancing in the direction of oncoming traffic.

Damn, but she was a looker. She was tall for a woman, he thought, probably around five foot seven or eight, very slender, with long legs and a delicate bone structure. Her face was heart-shaped, with high cheekbones and finely arched brows.

And her mouth, Lord. Wide and lush and curved at the corners.

He sighed with disappointment. She was business, he reminded himself, not pleasure.

But hey, he thought, snatching his keys from his ignition. A guy can look, can't he?

He slipped out of his car, careful not to make eye contact with her as he casually stepped off the curb. It appeared that she was waiting for a ride and he'd have to move fast or she'd get away. He was halfway across the street when she turned suddenly, then walked quickly in the opposite direction and disappeared around the corner.

Dammit!

Had she seen him? he wondered. He didn't think so, and even if she had, she couldn't possibly know he was coming for her. He sprinted to the corner, then looked down the street. There were people out walking, business men and women headed for lunch and shoppers coming out and going into stores, but no sign of Clair Beauchamp.

What the hell? Had she gone into another store? Clenching his jaw, he was about to head for the closest shop, Maiman's Jewelers, when he spotted the arched brick walkway leading to an inner court. The scent of grilling hamburgers and freshly made pizza drifted from the corridor.

Letting instinct lead him, Jacob ducked into the walkway and followed it into an inner, open-air court-yard heavy with ferns and fountains. Lunch diners sat at wrought-iron tables and chairs in the center of the shaded court where vendors served everything from sandwiches to hot dogs.

Gotcha.

She stood in front of a corner cart where a freckled-faced young man was too busy staring at his pretty customer to pay attention to the money she was counting out. When she looked up at the moon-eyed kid, he turned bright red, then handed her a plump hot dog smothered in ketchup and mustard. Jacob shook his head with amusement, then ducked behind a fern when she glanced over her shoulder in his direction. He watched as she walked a few feet away and stood with her back to him.

"Show time," Jacob muttered under his breath.

He came up behind her, stopped three feet away to give her a little space. "Clair Beauchamp?"

She jumped, and without turning around, pitched the hot dog into the trash can. Puzzled, Jacob watched as she straightened her shoulders and turned.

"Yes?"

Damn. She might be business, but his pulse still leaped when she faced him. He thought she'd looked good from across the street, but close up she was lethal.

"Miss Beauchamp, I—" He paused, then looked at the trash can and frowned. "Why did you do that?"

"Do what?"

Annoyed, he gestured toward the trash can. "Throw a perfectly good hot dog away."

"I have no idea what you're talking about." Lifting her pretty chin, she slid her sunglasses down her nose. "Do I know you?"

Oh, she was good, Jacob thought. Just the right amount of disdain in her soft Southern voice and impatience in her piercing blue gaze to put him in his place without being overly rude. What the hell. What did he care if she'd tossed the damn hot dog? No skin off his nose.

"My name is Jacob Carver." He pulled out his P.I. badge and flashed it at her. "I've been hired by a lawyer's firm in Wolf River, Texas, to contact you."

She leaned closer and took a look at his badge, then slid her sunglasses back up. "Whatever for?"

"Can we sit?" He nodded at an empty table a few feet away.

"I'm afraid not, Mr. Carver. I'm already late for a lunch meeting." She flipped open the catch on her purse, then smoothly retrieved a card and handed it to him. "If you call this number, my mother's secretary will set up an appointment. Now if you'll excuse me—"

"Miss Beauchamp." He moved and blocked her path, watched her lips press together in annoyance. "My employer insists that I speak to you and only to you."

"And I insist that you let me pass."

"I only want five minutes." He smiled and spread his hands. "You don't need to be afraid. I'm not here to hurt you."

"I'm not afraid," she said icily. "I'm in a hurry."

But the fact was, Clair thought, she *was* afraid. And though she was used to people approaching her, usually for a donation to a charity or a request for an endorsement, it wasn't every day a man sneaked up behind her, caught her completely off guard, then cornered her.

And he wasn't just *any* man, she thought, holding her purse tightly to her chest. He had to be the most *rugged* man she'd ever seen. The navy-blue T-shirt he wore hugged his muscular upper torso, while faded denim stretched across his long legs. He'd neglected to cut his dark hair for some time and his face—a face that had made her breath catch when she'd first turned around—hadn't seen the sharp end of a razor for a couple of days, either. His eyes were almost as dark as his hair, his nose bent at the bridge and his mouth—her gaze dropped there now—his mouth had a devil-take-you arrogance that made her throat go dry.

Straightening her shoulders, she tried to push past him. "I'm sorry, but I really can't—"

Once again he blocked her. "Have you ever heard the names Jonathan and Norah Blackhawk?"

"No. And I would appreciate—"

"What about Rand and Seth Blackhawk?"

She faltered, had to blink back the unexpected and sudden pain behind her eyes. She'd never heard any of those names before, she was certain she hadn't. And yet...

Rand and Seth...

She shook her head. "Why would I?"

"Because—" Jacob leaned down and inched his face closer to hers "—Jonathan and Norah Blackhawk are your real parents, and Rand and Seth are your brothers.''

She stared at him for what felt like an eternity, then started to laugh. "That's the most ridiculous thing I've ever heard."

But he didn't smile, just kept that dark, somber gaze locked on her face. "Jonathan and Norah were killed in a car accident in Wolf River twenty-three years ago. Their three children were in the car, as well, but they survived the accident and were split up. Rand, age nine, was adopted by Edward and Mary Sloan in San Antonio. Seth, age seven, was adopted by Ben and Susan Granger, in New Mexico. Elizabeth Marie, age two, was adopted by Charles and Josephine Beauchamp, from South Carolina, but living in France at the time. You and Elizabeth, Miss Beauchamp, are one and the same."

The smile on her lips died, and the pain behind her eyes intensified. "This is either a bad joke, Mr. Carver, or you're a bad private investigator who's made a very big mistake."

"This is no joke," he said, shaking his head. "And I don't make mistakes. You were born Elizabeth Marie Blackhawk, adopted illegally by the Beauchamps while they were living in France. When Charles and Josephine returned to the States a year later with a three-year-old baby girl and told everyone you were their daughter, no one questioned their story."

White spots swam in front of her eyes, and the sounds of people talking and laughing suddenly seemed very far away. "I—I don't believe you."

"Come, sit down." His voice was gentle as he touched her arm. "Just for a minute."

Dazed, she let him lead her to a table where he

pulled a chair out for her. She started to sit, then shook her head. "No. This is *ridiculous*." She jerked her arm from his hand. "I *do not* believe you!"

Heads turned. Clair didn't look at them, didn't care. What did it matter if a hundred people stared? A thousand? The man—Jacob—reached into his back pocket, pulled out some folded papers, then handed them to her.

"I realize you need some time to think about this, Miss Beauchamp. These documents will explain what happened. Read them, ask your parents for the truth. Call me when you're ready."

The papers in his hand might as well have been snakes. She couldn't touch them, *wouldn't* touch them.

With a sigh, he slipped them into her shopping bag. Her heart pounded in her chest and the pain behind her eyes became unbearable.

She had to get out of here. Now.

She turned and ran…and did not look back.

"Clair, darling, please open the door. Please, baby."

Clair lay on her bed inside her locked bedroom and ignored her mother's persistent knocking. She'd been standing in the hallway for fifteen minutes, pleading, threatening, even crying, but Clair had refused to answer.

"I know you're in there, sweetheart. Talk to me. Tell me what's wrong. Your daddy and I will fix it."

Holding the papers that Jacob Carver had given her, Clair stared at the ceiling. The documents were from a lawyer named Henry Barnes: a copy of a birth certificate, a newspaper article describing the car accident, a photograph—enlarged and scanned—of Norah Blackhawk in a hospital bed holding a newborn, surrounded by her smiling family: a handsome husband and two little boys.

Clair had stared at the photograph for the past hour. Norah Blackhawk looked so much like herself, she thought. The same hair, the same high cheekbones, the same blue eyes.

And the most damning evidence of all, a copy of a contract between a lawyer named Leon Waters in Granite Springs and Charles and Josephine Beauchamp, a vague agreement to exchange an undisclosed amount of money if a certain "package" met with their approval.

Clair had come straight home after the P.I. Jacob had sucker punched her with this information. She hadn't believed anything the man told her, she *still* didn't believe it.

How could it be possible? How could any of this have happened? And why would her parents have done such a thing?

"Oh, Charles, thank God you're here," Clair heard her mother say on the other side of the door. "She was supposed to meet Victoria and me for lunch, but she never showed so I called the house and Tiffany said that she came in over an hour ago, looking as if she'd seen a ghost. She wouldn't speak to Tiffany or Richard, just went straight to her room and now she won't open the door."

"Clair, this is your father!" A heavy knock rattled the walls. "Open this door at once! I haven't time for this nonsense."

With a sigh, Clair sat. She knew she wouldn't be

able to hold her father off for long. She was going to have to face her parents and it might as well be now.

A knot twisted in her stomach as she stood, and she stared at the papers still in her hand.

Jonathan and Norah Blackhawk are your real parents…killed in a car accident…Rand and Seth…

Rand and Seth. Those names meant something to her. Something important.

She sucked in a breath and swallowed hard. Whatever the truth was, whatever it was that happened twenty-three years ago, she had to know.

"Clair Louise! Open up immed—"

Her father's fist was in the air, ready to knock again, as Clair opened the door. Wide-eyed, her mother rushed forward.

"Clair, baby!" Her mother hugged her.

"What's happened?" her father demanded.

Her body stiff, Clair pulled away from her mother's embrace, then stepped aside. "Mother, Father. Come in and sit down, please."

It amazed Clair how calm her voice sounded, how calm *she* actually felt.

"What's gotten into you?" Charles frowned. "Your mother dragged me away from a meeting, insisting you were ill. I demand to know what's going on."

"Stop yelling at her, Charles." Josephine waved a dismissive hand at her husband. "Can't you see she's already upset?"

"Mother—"

"Clair, sugar." Josephine reached out and cupped Clair's face in her hands. "All brides are nervous before their wedding. It's perfectly normal. Charles, run and get my sedatives from the medicine—"

"No!"

Charles and Josephine both went still. Clair had never spoken to her parents in that tone of voice in her entire life. She couldn't even remember if she'd ever said no to them.

"Clair, you're frightening me." Her mother clasped a hand to her throat. "What is it? What's—"

"Wolf River."

"Wolf River?" Josephine whispered, then glanced at her husband.

And in that second, in that space between heartbeats, between breaths, Clair knew it was true.

Dear God.

Josephine's deep-brown eyes filled with panic. She made a move toward her daughter, but Clair held out a hand and shook her head.

"It's true." Clair felt her heart slam against her ribs and her pulse pound in her head. "I *am* adopted."

Charles pressed his mouth into a firm line. "Where did you hear such a thing?"

For the past hour, she'd been praying that someone had been playing a horrible joke on her, or that the private investigator had made a mistake.

I don't make mistakes, he'd told her.

Based on her parents' expressions, it appeared that he was right.

Her throat felt like dust, and when she finally found the words to speak, her voice was barely a whisper. "A man named Jacob Carver, a private investigator hired by a lawyer from Wolf River, approached me when I came out of Evelyn's. He gave me a newspaper article about the car accident and a photograph of my birth parents and two brothers.'' Clair held up the papers in her hand. ''He also gave me a copy of a document, an agreement between you and a man named Leon Waters.''

Josephine gasped, then reached for her husband's arm to steady herself. ''Clair—''

''He told me my name—my real name—is Elizabeth Marie.'' Clair moved to her bedroom window, stared out at the sprawling front lawn of the estate where she'd been raised. It was green and lush, surrounded by neat rows of thick azaleas and tall crepe myrtles. The house, a two-story brick tudor, with ten bedrooms and a grand, sweeping staircase guaranteed to present the most proper, the most elegant, and the most impressive entrance to any party, was the largest in the wealthy neighborhood.

''My...parents' names were Jonathan and Norah Blackhawk. Jonathan was Cherokee and Norah was Welsh.''

''Please, come sit down,'' Charles said tightly. ''We need to talk about this.''

Clair turned sharply from the window. ''You *bought* me. Just like one of your ships or houses or cars.''

''For God's sake, Clair.'' Charles shook his head. ''You're overdramatizing. It wasn't like that at all.''

She held the papers to her stomach as if they were a shield. ''Then why don't you tell me what it *was* like?''

''Charles, please, let me.'' Josephine looked up at her husband and squeezed his arm. When he nodded, she turned her gaze back to her daughter. ''Shortly after your father and I were married, his business partner in Paris offered to sell his interest in the company.

Though it meant moving to France for a few years and being away from the States, we both knew it was an opportunity we couldn't let pass. It was a busy time for your father, and I was alone a great deal of the time. Two years later, when we found out I was pregnant, we were both thrilled.''

Josephine moved to Clair's bed and sank down on the edge. ''I miscarried at five months. There were complications. I...I had to have a hysterectomy when I was only twenty-eight.'' Josephine closed her eyes. ''I thought my life was over.''

Through her own cloud of confusion and anger, Clair's heart ached for her mother. She moved to the bed and sat beside her. There were tears in Josephine's eyes when she opened them again.

''When your father brought you home to me—'' Josephine reached up and tucked a loose strand of hair behind Clair's ear ''—I didn't ask how he found you. I didn't care. All I knew was that you were the most beautiful child I'd ever seen, the most perfect little girl in the whole world, and you belonged to me. You were three when we came back to the States and since we'd been gone for over four years, there were never any questions.''

''Mr. Carver said the adoptions were illegal.'' Clair looked at her father. ''That a lawyer named Leon Waters sold me to you.''

''That vile man,'' Josephine said with a shudder. ''I never would have known his name if he hadn't called six months after you came to live with us. He threatened to take you away from us if we didn't give him more money. We gave him what he wanted, and then your father told me the truth after everything. About Wolf River and how your family had died.''

"Mr. Carver said my brothers didn't die." Clair handed the photograph of her birth family to her mother. "That they live in Texas and they want to meet me."

Josephine shook her head. "That's not true. There were death certificates on record for your brothers. Your father told me he saw them."

"But the newspaper—" she drew in a deep, steadying breath "—the article said that the *entire* Blackhawk family was killed."

"The lawyer assured me that was an error by an incompetent reporter," Charles stated firmly. "Waters knew that I wanted to adopt without going through months—if not years—of paperwork, so when you were brought to him, he didn't bother to correct the newspaper. He called me, I flew to the States, then I brought you back to France with me."

"Clair." Josephine took her daughter's hand. "This man, this Jacob Carver, is lying about your brothers. He must have found out what happened and he wants money. That's the only explanation why after all these years this has come to the surface."

Clair shook her head. "He didn't ask me for money."

"Not yet, but he will." Josephine's face was ashen, her voice trembling. "A scandal like this three days before your wedding? He knows we'd do anything to keep this quiet for now. Promise me you won't speak to him again."

"I, I don't know. I'm not—"

"Sweetheart." Josephine's chest rose on a sob. "Even if I didn't carry you in my womb, you're my little girl and I love you so very much. Please, Clair, forgive us for keeping the truth from you, and please,

please tell me you won't speak to that awful man again.''

Maybe she's right, Clair thought. Considering everything she'd just learned, she supposed it was possible that Jacob Carver was lying, that he was looking for some easy money. The P.I. *had* been a bit rough around the edges. And even though he hadn't appeared to be a blackmailer, you certainly couldn't look at a person and know what was going on inside.

She, of all people, knew how true that was.

Numb, Clair settled into the warmth of Josephine's embrace. This was the only mother she knew, the mother who'd played dress-up and dolls with her when she was little, brought her soup when she'd been sick, then tucked her in bed every night. The mother who'd fussed over her first date, cried at her high school and college graduation, worried when she came home too late.

Sooner or later, Clair knew that she would have to deal with the overwhelming reality of being adopted and the fact her parents had lied to her. It was too big, too *huge,* to be avoided or ignored.

And so was the fact that in seventy-six hours, thirty-three minutes and twenty-one seconds, Clair Louise Beauchamp was getting married.

Arms crossed, Jacob leaned against a thick marble column in the back of the one-hundred-eighty-five-year-old cathedral. Huge sprays of white and pink roses filled the church. A quartet played Handel's water music while at least two hundred smiling, murmuring people sat watching a blond bridesmaid dressed in satin turquoise float down an aisle long enough to land a Cessna.

Jacob wondered what those two hundred people would be murmuring if they'd seen Blondie and Oliver slipping out of the Wanderlust Motel at 1:00 a.m. for the past two nights. Most likely they'd be wishing they hadn't had their present engraved.

It had been completely by coincidence that Jacob had discovered Clair's husband-to-be's little peccadillo. Since Jacob hadn't been able to get close to Clair's gated estate, he'd decided to follow her fiancé instead, hoping the prospective groom might somehow lead him to Clair.

Only it wasn't Clair that Oliver Hollingsworth met at the seedy motel just outside of town. It was Blondie. Out of habit, Jacob had snapped a few pictures, but he'd have no use for them. He wasn't here to catch a philandering fiancé or husband. He was here to convince Clair to speak with her brothers, or better, to meet with them.

He'd thought for certain that she would have called him after he'd given her the documents proving his story was true. Though he'd just met her, and barely spoken to her for more than a few minutes, there was something about Clair that made him think she was different from that rich, snobby crowd her family ran with. When she hadn't known he was watching her, there'd been something in her eyes, something in her expression, that set her apart.

Obviously he'd been wrong.

At the sound of the quartet playing the "Wedding March," Jacob straightened. Two hundred heads turned in the direction of the door where the bride would be entering the cathedral.

Damn. So much for catching the bride alone for five seconds. Once she walked down that aisle, it would be days, probably weeks, before he'd be able to get close to her again.

Damn, damn.

He watched the side door at the back of the church open, then, for one long, heart-stopping moment, he simply couldn't think at all. Like a white cloud, Clair Beauchamp floated toward him, her face covered by her veil.

Oliver Hollingsworth might be a two-timing jerk, Jacob thought, but he was one hell of a lucky two-timing jerk.

Clair might have kept her carefully paced stride steady and even, might have kept her shoulders straight and her chin level, might have even remembered to breathe—if she hadn't seen Jacob Carver leaning casually against a marble column when she'd come out of the bride's anteroom.

He wore black—T-shirt, jeans, boots—and Clair thought he looked like the devil himself. When he grinned at her and touched two fingers to his temple, her step faltered and her icy hands clutched desperately at the elegant bouquet of white roses.

How dare he show up here! At her wedding, with two hundred guests in attendance. And how dare he look at her with such accusation in his eyes, such reproach.

So she hadn't called him. Why should she? After twenty-three years, what difference did it make now that she'd been adopted? Her parents loved her. Oliver loved her. They had a wonderful, happy life ahead of them.

Only a few feet away, her father held out a hand to her. She glanced at him, then at Oliver, who stood at the front of the church, watching her, smiling calmly, waiting.

Oh, God.

Her heart pounding fiercely, Clair stepped up to her father and looked into his eyes. "Daddy, I—I'm sorry."

With a sigh, Charles dropped his chin, then nodded. "It's all right, baby." He leaned forward and kissed her on the cheek. "Do what you have to do."

"Thank you," she whispered through the lump in her throat, then handed the bouquet to her father and hugged him. "Tell Mom I love her."

She heard the murmur from the pews behind her as she turned and walked briskly toward Jacob. Lifting her chin, she met his dark gaze with her own.

"Mr. Carver," she said politely. "May I trouble you for a ride?"

Two

While the sun rode low on a silver-streaked horizon, they drove in silence. Past sprawling, two-story colonial estates. Past a thoroughbred farm with long, white fences and sleek, shiny horses grazing in thick, green grass. Past a restored antebellum mansion that was now a hotel and spa.

Clair stared straight ahead, back perfectly straight, her long, elegant neck held high. She clasped her slender hands tightly together in her lap. Between her billowing skirts and the fountain of sheer white netting that covered her head, she literally filled the front seat of his car. The sweet, delicate scent of roses still clung to her gown.

Jacob checked his rear view mirror for the tenth time, was relieved to see that no one had followed them. Pushing her skirt out of his way, he shifted gears and pulled down a quiet, tree-lined neighborhood of old, but elegant brick homes, then parked his car under the shade of a spreading magnolia. He shut off the engine, rolled down his window, then reached across Clair and rolled hers down, as well. She didn't flinch, didn't move. Didn't speak.

On the same side of the street, a white-haired gentleman strolled toward them with a Pekinese on the end of a leash. Both man and dog glanced over as they approached, and the old guy's eyes went soft with admiration as he stared at the vintage car. When he caught sight of Clair, the man lifted a curious brow and then shrugged and moved on.

Clair didn't even notice.

"Clair."

He said her name gently, shifted his body in his seat and looked at her. She sat stiff as a preacher's collar, unblinking, her lips pressed into a thin line.

"Clair."

His gaze dropped to her chest to see if she was breathing. Based on the shallow rise and fall of her breasts, he determined she was. And because he was only human, he took a moment to appreciate the view before he said her name more sharply.

"Clair."

She blinked. Her blue eyes wide, she slowly turned to look at him.

"You want to tell me what happened back there?" he asked.

"I—" She stopped, swallowed, then glanced away. "I just ran out on my fiancé, my parents and two hundred guests."

He'd pretty much figured that part out. Now to ask the next, most logical question. "Why?"

"I didn't love him." Her voice quivered. She

turned back and leveled her gaze with his. "I...didn't *love* him."

The second time she said it, her voice was stronger and didn't waver. Jacob leaned back against his car door and studied her, decided that maybe his first assessment of her had been right, after all. Maybe there *was* something different about Clair.

"And you just realized that now?"

She stared at the sparkling diamond on her hand. "I've known Oliver most of my life. Our families spent holidays together, celebrated birthdays and anniversaries. It made my parents so happy when he proposed. It never occurred to me to turn him down."

"Until today."

"My entire life has been a lie." She slipped the ring off her finger and laid it in the palm of her hand. "My parents lied to me. I lied to myself and to Oliver. All because we were afraid to tell the truth, afraid of the consequences. When I walked out and looked at all those people sitting in the church, then saw you, I knew it was now or never."

Her fingers closed around the ring. "They'll never forgive me."

He'd liked to tell her that she'd made the right decision, that her fiancé had been doing the mattress mambo with one of her so-called friends. But he could see the cold fear in her eyes, the heavy guilt. He sure as hell didn't want to be the one to add to the woman's grief.

And besides, Clair Beauchamp's love life wasn't his problem. He'd been hired to find her, not rescue her.

"My parents confirmed everything you said about my birth family." From a pocket at her hip, she pulled out a white silk handkerchief, folded the ring inside, then tucked it back into the dress. "Except they told me that my brothers were dead, that they died in the accident along with my parents. My father saw the death certificates for Rand and Seth."

"The death certificates were phonies," Jacob said. "And so was yours."

She swiveled a look at him, blinked. "Mine?"

Jacob nodded.

"I see." Frowning, she touched a shaking hand to her temple and shook her head. "No, actually, I don't see at all. How could this be possible? How could a family be separated like we were and adopted out, legal or illegal? Why didn't anyone know?"

"The lawyer in Wolf River will explain everything." Jacob pulled his cell phone out of his shirt pocket. "You can talk to your brothers and—"

"No."

He stopped dialing and looked up at her. "No?"

"No. Not on the phone."

"All right." Jacob set the phone down. "I'll drive you to your house, you can pack a few things, then I'll put you on a plane to Dallas. Wolf River is about three hours from the airport and someone will—"

"Mr. Carver, the last place I'd go right now is home. And I have no intention of getting on a plane."

Clair wasn't certain when she'd actually made that decision. Maybe two seconds ago, or maybe the moment she'd seen Jacob in the church. Either way, it didn't matter.

She was *not* going home.

"First of all," he said on an exhale, "why don't you just call me Jacob?"

Clair felt her breath catch when his gaze slid slowly

over her. Something in those dark eyes of his sent a strange shiver up her spine.

Good Lord, it was hot in his car.

"Second…" His gaze came back up to meet hers. "Just in just you forgot, you're still in your wedding dress."

"I assure you, Jacob, *no one* could *possibly* be more aware of what I'm wearing than me." The dress had been made to fit like a glove and it was squeezing the breath out of her. It was squeezing the *life* out of her. "But I'm not going home."

"Oookaay." He draped an arm over his steering wheel. "And your plan is?"

"Quite simple, really." It had taken her mother fifteen minutes to get her veil anchored to her head in the church dressing room. It took Clair two seconds to rip it out. "You'll drive me to Wolf River."

He stared at her for a full five seconds. "Excuse me?"

"I said—" she did her best to ignore the horrific itch between her tightly bound breasts "—I'd like you to drive me to Wolf River."

"Not possible." He shook his head. "I was hired to find you and make contact. I'm sorry, but my job is finished now."

"Then I'm rehiring you." She rolled her shoulders back, but it did nothing to relieve the unbearable itch. "What's your fee?"

"You're actually serious?" His laugh was short and dry. "It doesn't matter what my fee is. I'll take you to the airport and get you on a plane, but that's all I can do."

"I'll double it."

She saw the hesitation in his eyes, the slight lift of one eyebrow, but then he shook his head again.

"Look," he said slowly, "I can appreciate you're a little upset at the moment and you're not thinking clearly, but—"

"Stop." She leaned in closer to him and narrowed her eyes. "Just stop right there. *You* show up three days ago and tell me my entire life has been a lie. I just walked out on the only family I've ever known, not to mention my fiancé and two hundred wedding guests. Do *not* tell me you can appreciate what I'm feeling or thinking at this moment. You can't possibly have a *clue* what's going on inside me right now."

Clair pressed a hand to her stomach, stunned that she'd actually raised her voice. Stunned to realize that it *felt good* to raise her voice. Still, a lifetime of strict manners and proper behavior had her quickly backtracking.

"I apologize." She straightened her shoulders and did her best to ignore the increasing itch across her chest. "That was rude of me. I'm sure we can discuss this in a calm manner."

"There's nothing to discuss."

When his gaze dropped to her breasts and lingered there, Clair felt a thrill lurch in her stomach. Good heavens, but the man was brazen! Even Oliver would never have stared so blatantly at her. She resisted the urge to cover herself with her hands. And scratch.

When his gaze did not lift, the thrill Clair had felt faded and turned to indignation. "Mr. Carver," she said, forcing a cool tone to her voice, "if you stopped staring at my chest, perhaps you could at least hear me out."

"Sorry. But that wasn't there a few minutes ago."

"What wasn't where?"

"That."

Clair glanced down and gasped. On her chest, spreading upward from her décolletage, was a trail of dime-size bright red splotches. Damn this miserable dress!

"That's gotta itch," he said.

"It's nothing," she lied. Her cheeks were as hot as her chest when she grabbed her veil and covered herself. She *wouldn't* scratch. "Mr. Car—Jacob—I need to go to Wolf River, but I also need a few days to absorb everything that's happened. I may not have any money on me at this moment, but I assure you, I have access to personal funds. Name your price."

Damn, but Clair Louise Beauchamp–Elizabeth-Marie Blackhawk was a haughty priss, Jacob thought. He couldn't decide if he was amused or annoyed. Maybe a little of both. But one thing was certain, she was one gorgeous haughty priss.

When she'd tugged her veil away from the sophisticated knot on top of her head, several strands of shiny dark hair had escaped and tumbled down her long, slender neck. Tear-shaped pearls dripped from her earlobes and a matching necklace hugged the base of her throat. She had eyes that flashed blue fire one minute and cold ice the next, and a mouth that could tempt a saint.

He was no saint.

"Look, Clair," he said impatiently. "Maybe you're right. Maybe you do need some time to think all this over. I could check you into a quiet resort somewhere, incognito. In a few days—"

"I have no desire or intention to hide away in a resort." She lifted her chin. "I know what I want.

Maybe for the first time in my life. I'll *triple* your fee.''

''I—'' He stumbled mentally as her offer sank in. ''Triple?''

''Please.'' She leaned across the seat, laid her fingers on his arm. ''Jacob, please.''

Her hand on his bare skin was as smooth and warm as her plea. He told himself the sudden drought in his throat was caused by the late-afternoon heat building inside his car. He watched her lips part softly as she stared imploringly at him and felt a jolt of desire slam into his gut.

Pressing his lips tightly together, he pulled away and shook his head. ''No. I'm sorry, but you'll have to—''

When Clair started to ring, Jacob realized his cell phone was somewhere underneath the thick cloud of her gown. She gasped when he burrowed his way through the yards of stiff tulle, then pulled his phone out from under her bottom. ''Carver here.''

''Jacob Carver, you son of a bitch!'' a man said at the other end of the line. ''I demand you return my fiancée to the church immediately!''

Jacob raised a brow and casually asked, ''To whom am I speaking?''

''You know damn well who you're speaking to,'' Oliver Hollingsworth yelled. ''Get back here now!''

''I'm a little busy at the moment,'' Jacob drawled. ''How 'bout I get back to you?''

Oliver's response had Jacob raising both brows. Clair chewed nervously on her lip.

''I won't be humiliated like this,'' Oliver screamed into the phone. ''You'll return Clair this minute or I'll have your license revoked. I'll sue you for every penny you have. I'll have you arrested and thrown in—''

"I've got your number." Jacob cut him off. "Room 16 at the Wanderlust Motel. Nice little place, though the walls are a little thin, don't you think?"

There was a long, tight silence at the other end of the line, then Oliver said quietly, "Look, Carver, I'll make it worth your while to keep that little bit of information between us. Say twenty-five thousand? Return Clair to the church immediately and there'll be another twenty thousand on top of that. After the ceremony, you and I can talk man-to-man and—''

Jacob hung up on him, then shut his phone off.

I'll make it worth your while. The bastard hadn't even asked about Clair, Jacob thought irritably. Hadn't asked if she was all right, or even to speak to her. Hollingsworth just wanted her back at the church so he wouldn't be humiliated.

"Who was that?" Clair asked anxiously.

"No one you know," Jacob said almost truthfully and watched her relax.

"Jacob, if you would just please reconsider my offer and—''

"Fine."

"Fine?"

"I'll do it."

"You will?"

"I said I would, didn't I?" he said tightly. "But we'll do this my way, you got that?"

"Of course."

She smiled at him so sweetly, with such innocence, he felt another slam of desire in his gut.

Dammit.

"We'll stop when I say, where I say," he added. "And I don't want a lot of chitchat."

Pressing her lips firmly together, she nodded.

"Buckle up."

She snapped her seat belt on—not an easy task, considering that dress of hers—then leaned back in the seat and stared straight ahead.

He looked at her—her perfect profile, her serene smile, her stunningly beautiful face—and thought he was looking at an angel.

Clenching his jaw, Jacob started the car and headed back toward the highway. If he was going to keep his hands off Clair—and he *would,* dammit—he needed to get to Wolf River as fast—and with as few stops—as possible.

For the next forty-five minutes, Clair did her best not to think about what she'd left behind. Though she had no regrets she hadn't married Oliver, she felt terribly, horribly guilty for leaving like she had. Even if he had never been especially romantic or passionate with her in the two years they'd formally dated, he still hadn't deserved to be abandoned at the altar.

She had no idea if he or Victoria would ever forgive her, or even speak to her again. Strange, but she was most upset at the thought of Victoria never speaking to her again than she was Oliver.

Clair knew her parents would weather the scandal, though certainly those seas would be rough for a while. Knowing she had her father's approval gave her comfort, but there was still her mother to contend with, to appease. The thought made the incessant itch on Clair's chest intensify. She squeezed her fingers into fists, did her best to concentrate on the passing greenery of the countryside and the wail of Aretha Franklin blasting from Jacob's car stereo.

She'd managed not to speak since Jacob had turned onto the highway, hadn't even asked him where they were going. He'd made no effort to speak at all, either. She'd tried counting red cars, then blue cars, then cars with four-doors versus two-doors, but she simply couldn't distract herself from what was currently, and most immediately, on her mind—

The overwhelming, overpowering, all-consuming need to scratch.

Damn, this miserable rash! She knew it was only nerves, but that certainly didn't ease her misery. She'd felt it spreading to her back, and with the way her dress seemed to be shrinking, her entire torso would be covered before long.

She wouldn't scratch…she wouldn't scratch…she wouldn't scratch…

"Stop the car!"

Jacob snapped his head around. "What?"

"Stop the car," she hissed through her teeth. "Now."

Frowning, he pulled off the highway and parked behind a stand of cypress trees. "Sweetheart, if you've changed your mind, then you're on your—"

She unbuckled her seat belt and turned her back to him, pressed a hand to her chest and felt the burning heat there. "Unbutton me."

"What?"

"Hurry!"

Under a more "normal" situation, a woman asking him to unbutton her dress and be quick about it would have been a compliment and a pleasure to Jacob. With Clair, however, the situation was anything but normal.

"Jacob, *please!*"

"All right, all right." Jacob stared at the back of Clair's dress. There were five tiny pearl buttons to release before the zipper could be pulled down. She wiggled under him while he struggled to unbutton her, and when he pulled the zipper down and the garment loosened around her, she let her head fall back and expelled a soft groan of delight.

"Now the corset."

His heart slammed against his ribs. *Oh, no…bad, bad idea…* "I don't really think I should be—"

"I can't do it myself." She squirmed, making the dress gape wider. "I swear I'll scream if I don't get out of this contraption immediately!"

Terrific. The last thing he needed was to be parked off the highway with a half-naked screaming woman. He reached for the top hook, then loosened each one until the stiff lace underwear fell away.

"Bless you," she sighed breathlessly, then sagged sideways against the seat.

Jacob winced at the sight of the red marks on her bare lower back. Her skin was blotchy, like her chest had been, and there were deep impressions from the too-tight corset. Without thinking, he reached out and laid his hand on her back. She jerked upright at the contact and stiffened.

"Relax," he said, lightly rubbing his palm over her hot skin. "I think I can manage to control myself, Clair. Just tell me where it itches."

"Right there." Her voice was strained, but she did settle back against the seat. "Everywhere."

Gently he moved his hand over her lower back, felt her slowly relax under his touch. When he slid his hand upward, she moaned softly and arched her spine against him, Jacob bit the inside of his mouth to hold back the threatening swear word.

Her skin felt like warm silk and he felt his own hand itch to explore, to slip deeper inside the dress and curve around her narrow waist. To slide his palm upward over her flat belly and feel the firm weight of her breast in his hand.

Her back, long and slender, was completely exposed to him. He felt an overwhelming desire to press his mouth to one smooth, bare shoulder and taste her, to nip at her warm skin.

"That feels wonderful," Clair breathed and snuggled against the car seat.

Clair had never experienced anything quite so relaxing—or *erotic*—in her life. Jacob's large hands moving slowly over her back were the most exquisite feeling in the world. His palms were rough, his fingers strong, yet gentle. Her entire body tingled at his touch, her skin felt unusually tight. Warm shivers of sheer pleasure coursed through her veins.

She felt as if she'd been drugged, or as if she'd just wakened from an intensely sensual dream and she was still trapped between fantasy and reality. Her limbs felt heavy, her mind sluggish.

It shocked her that she would allow this man she barely knew to touch her in such an intimate manner. Shocked her that she *wanted* him to touch her, to keep touching her, not only on her back, but other places, too. Her breasts ached to be touched, her nipples tightened. And lower, between her thighs, she felt a heavy warmth and a dull throb.

When his hands slid up her waist and his fingertips were no more than an inch from the underside of her breast, she felt her heart skip a beat, then start to pound furiously. She knew she should move away, but she couldn't. She *couldn't*.

Breath held, eyes closed, she felt him lean closer, felt the warmth of his breath on her shoulder...

And then, just as suddenly, he pulled her dress back up to cover her shoulders and moved away.

"Better?" he asked.

Too embarrassed to turn around and look at him, she simply nodded.

He said nothing, but she heard him open the car door, then step out. Thankful for the moment alone, she covered her face with her hands and groaned. She could only imagine what he must think of her. Not only had she begged him to unhook her dress, she'd allowed—no, *welcomed*—his touch.

She heard him rooting around in his trunk, and when he slammed it shut and came back around the car, she reached behind her to hold her dress together.

He stood outside the driver's door and tossed some clothing into the front seat. "Put these on for now. We'll find something more suitable when we stop for the night."

Clair glanced at the gray sweatpants and plain white T-shirt and looked up at Jacob. "I—thank you."

"You've got five minutes to change, then I'm getting back in this car whether you're dressed or not. I suggest you hurry."

He closed the door, then leaned up against the driver's door, arms crossed. Clair stared at his stiff back for a full ten seconds, then looked at the clothing. They'd be huge on her, but anything was better than this miserable dress.

Five minutes he'd given her, then he was getting

back in the car. Realizing she'd already wasted twenty seconds, she scrambled out of her wedding dress and corset and tossed them in the back seat, yanked the T-shirt over her head, then kicked her satin pumps off. She'd barely tugged the sweatpants over her hips when Jacob climbed back in the car and started the engine.

A plume of dirt sprayed behind them as he headed back to the highway. He held the steering wheel in a death grip and squealed onto the road as if the devil himself were on his heels. When he shifted gears and gunned the motor, the car leapt forward like a beast loosened from its cage.

With the church and her wedding behind her and the long road ahead, Clair felt a giddy sense of freedom she'd never experienced before. Smiling, she snapped her seat belt on, settled back, then mentally sang along with an Eagles' tune blasting from the radio.

Take It Easy...take it easy...

Three

It was nearly eight o'clock when Jacob pulled into the hamburger drive-thru stand. He was hungry, tired and in one hell of a bad mood.

He was used to traveling alone. He *liked* traveling alone. It hadn't mattered that Clair had managed to keep quiet for the entire time they'd been on the road. He couldn't relax, couldn't concentrate with a one-hundred-twenty-pound bundle of female sitting next to him. He'd kept his eyes off her and on the road, but he'd felt the energy radiating from her, felt her excitement, her nervousness, her anxiety.

And if that wasn't enough to drive him crazy, he could smell her. That incredible, tantalizing scent that kept reminding him how soft her skin had been under his hands, how smooth. Reminded him how much he'd wanted to touch her all over. With his hands and his mouth and—

"Welcome to Bobby Burgers in the beautiful town of Lenore, South Carolina. My name is Tiffany," a perky teenager bubbled through the speaker static of the drive-thru stand. "May I take your order, please?"

He dragged a hand through his hair, then stuck his head out of the window. "We'll have three Big Bob's, two fries and two—"

"Wait, wait, wait." Clair unbuckled her seat belt. "Let me look."

"What's to look at?" he said irritably when she scooted across the seat.

Pleasure lit her eyes as she stared at the menu. "Chili fries," she said with reverence. "I want one of those, please."

Shaking his head, Jacob turned back to the speaker. "Make that a—"

"Wait, wait, wait." She leaned over him, placed a hand on his arm. "With extra cheese. Oh, and a chocolate shake."

She was practically in his lap. He could feel the warmth of her body, and the knowledge she had no bra on under his T-shirt had Jacob grinding his teeth. "Is that all?"

"Maybe some extra pickles and mayonnaise on the hamburger. Oh, and some of those little green spicy things, too, please."

"Jalapeños?"

She smiled brightly and nodded. "That's it. On the side."

They picked up their order, then he pulled the car into the hamburger stand's parking lot and handed Clair her cache. She pulled several napkins out of the greasy brown paper bag and spread them over her lap.

Jacob watched with interest as she opened her burger and took a small, delicate bite. She closed her eyes with a sigh and smiled.

"I take it you like Bobby's Burgers," he said, and tore into his own hamburger.

"This is my first." She pulled out a jalapeño and stuck it between the meat and her bun.

"Your first Bobby's Burger?" He stared at her in disbelief. "They have twenty-five thousand franchises in fifty states," he quoted the sign. "*Everyone* has eaten a Bobby's Burger."

"I haven't." She took a bite, then sucked in a breath as she waved her hand in front of her mouth. There were tears in her eyes.

Grinning, he handed her the chocolate shake she'd ordered. She took a long sip, then settled back in her seat and reached for a chili-covered French fry.

"My mother had a very specific list of foods our chef was allowed to prepare." She ate the French fry as delicately as her burger. "Hamburger was on the forbidden list."

"So that's why you pitched the hot dog in the trash can." He reached for his soda. "You thought I was one of your mother's spies."

"Something like that." Clair chewed thoughtfully. "My mother worries."

"About hamburgers and hot dogs?"

"You don't even want to know." She sighed, then stared thoughtfully at another French fry. "Sometimes she's a little overprotective."

"A *little* overprotective?" Jacob snorted and took a gulp of soda. "That's like saying Shaquille O'Neil is a little tall."

Clair lifted her chin. "It's only because she loves

me. I was—am—her only child. I'm sure your mother worries about you, too.''

''My mother worried so much she left me and my younger brother with an alcoholic father when I was nine,'' he said without emotion. ''She did manage to show up at my dad's funeral when I was eighteen, but only because she'd found out she was the beneficiary of a small life insurance policy. She collected her money and I haven't seen her since.''

''I'm sorry,'' Clair said quietly, lifting her gaze to his. ''It appears we come from two extremes.''

''Sweetheart—'' he raised his drink to her ''—that's the understatement of the century.''

They finished their meal in silence, and he had to admit he was more than a little surprised that Clair managed to polish off the food she'd ordered, including the peppers.

He watched her long, slender fingers smooth and fold the paper from her burger, flatten the foam cup her fries had been in, then place everything back in the brown paper bag. It was like watching a ballet, he decided. She moved with the grace and fluidity of a dancer, and the fact she was dressed in an oversize T-shirt and baggy sweats didn't detract from her elegance in the slightest.

Still, no matter how well she wore his clothes, he realized she would need something more suitable for their trip, not to mention a few personal items.

There was no getting around it, Jacob thought with a silent groan. He was going to have to do something he *dreaded*. Something he *swore* he'd never do.

His palms started to sweat at the very thought of it.

He was going to take a woman shopping.

* * *

Two hours later, Clair sat in the middle of her motel room floor and pulled her treasures out of the plastic Sav-Mart shopping bags. A pretty pink cotton tank top, a short denim skirt, a mint-green button-up blouse. She hadn't tried anything on, but she had bags and bags of clothes in front of her. Smiling, she picked up a soft lavender sweater and held it to her cheek.

Every single item she'd chosen completely by herself. She'd never been in a Sav-Mart Department store before, though she'd heard of them. After all, they were the largest discount department store in the country. But Josephine Beauchamp would never have been caught dead in a Sav-Mart. If she knew that her daughter had not only gone to the huge chain store, but bought an entire wardrobe off the racks, she would be hyperventilating. And if she'd seen what her daughter had *worn* to go shopping there—a man's T-shirt, sweatpants and satin pumps—Good Lord, she'd need smelling salts to recover.

Though certainly Clair had felt more than a little self-conscious about her attire when she'd first entered the store, she'd quickly forgotten her discomfort once Jacob had grabbed a shopping cart and headed for the women's section. She'd followed along behind him, trying to keep up with his long strides, while taking in the experience at the same time.

Everything about the warehouse-style shopping had absolutely fascinated Clair. Aisles that seemed as long as a football field, heavily stocked six-foot-high shelves. Huge bins filled with a fascinating assortment of discounted items. Bicycles, trash cans, pet food, patio furniture, books—everything under the same roof.

Jacob stopped at the women's section, folded those muscular arms across that broad chest of his, assumed a sour expression, then told her to be quick about it.

Clair had always shopped in exclusive specialty stores with designer labels and tailored, custom-made clothing. But here there were racks and racks of ready-to-wear clothes. Dresses, blouses, skirts, underwear, night wear, shoes. Jacob had complained that she'd grabbed at least one of everything, but he'd paid for everything with his credit card, and she'd assured him that he would be reimbursed in full.

She'd filled the cart with clothes, spent another thirty minutes in the toiletries-and-cosmetics section, where she'd also bought nearly one of everything, including a jar of iridescent glitter body cream and a tube of sparkling, liquid blue eye shadow. Jacob had driven to the motel when she'd finished shopping, and she'd waited in the car while he registered them for two rooms. Grumbling and growling the entire time, he'd grabbed her shopping bags and the suitcase she'd picked out, then helped her into her room. Clair was certain he hadn't said more than three words since they'd left the store.

She couldn't imagine what his problem was, and at the moment she really didn't care.

She was too busy having fun.

Dizzy with delight, she reached for the bag filled with the assortment of underwear she'd picked out. She'd been thankful that Jacob had occupied himself with a sports magazine on the other side of the register while she'd emptied the shopping cart onto the register conveyer belt. If it hadn't been embarrassing enough to watch the young male clerk pick up and scan her undergarments, he'd also had to yell at another employee for a price check on one of the bras. Clair had forced herself to stand there calmly, though inside she'd wished that the floor would open up and swallow her whole.

Amazingly, she'd survived, and now, sitting cross-legged, she laid everything out in front of her: bras and panties in black lace and white silk and flowered satin. Push-up, sheer, embroidered, strapless—she'd shown no restraint.

And last, but not least, she pulled her most daring purchase of the evening out of the bag—one leopard-print thong panty.

She couldn't wait to try it on.

Gathering everything into her arms, she stood quickly and started for the bathroom. Halfway there, she paused at the first rumble of pain in her stomach.

The knock on the door came at the same time the second pain hit. Sucking in a breath, she set the lingerie on the bed, then carefully, slowly moved toward the door and opened it. Jacob stood on the other side.

He looked at her, then furrowed his brow. "You okay?"

"I—" The pain eased off, though the nausea lingered. "Yes. I'm fine."

"You look a little pale."

"Just a twinge in my stomach. Nerves, I'm sure," she said, drawing in a deep breath. "I'm all right now."

"You sure?"

"I'm fine. Really."

"Good." He held out a sweet-smelling pink box and opened the lid. "I bought some doughnuts across the street. I figured you might want one now or in the morning.''

If she'd been pale a second before, Clair's face turned sheet-white as she stared at the box. Jacob watched her clamp a hand over her mouth, spin on her bare heels and dash for the bathroom. She slammed the door behind her.

Uh-oh.

So much for doughnuts.

He snagged a maple bar for himself, then moved into her room and closed the door behind him. There were bags and articles of clothing everywhere, which hardly surprised him since he'd not only had to suffer the shopping ordeal, he'd hauled all the bags into her room. You'd have thought she was going on a six-month cruise, he thought, taking a big bite of the sugary doughnut. He lifted a brow at the undergarments she'd tossed on the bed. Her choice of lingerie had been the more interesting part of the shopping trip, though he'd pretended not to notice one way or the other what she'd thrown into the Sav-Mart basket. But, hey—he took another bite of doughnut—a guy couldn't completely ignore racy black lace bras and skimpy matching panties, now, could he?

Stepping beside the bed, he picked up the leopard print and nearly choked on his last bite of doughnut.

Good Lord, she'd bought a *thong*.

His heart skipped, then raced as he stared at the tiny scrap of silk. The last thing he needed was an image of thong underwear on Clair. For that matter, he didn't need—or want—an image of Clair in *any* underwear.

No, wait—he shook his head—that wasn't what he meant, either, dammit.

Thankfully the sound of the toilet flushing was like ice water on his wandering thoughts. He dropped the thong back onto the bed, licked the sugar crust off his thumb, then moved to the bathroom door.

"You okay?" He knocked lightly.

"I'm fine," she said weakly. "Go away, please."

Ignoring her request, he opened the door and stepped into the bathroom. She sat on the cool, white tile floor, her back against the tub, her forehead resting on her bent knees. He pulled a washcloth off the towel rack, ran it under cold water, then handed it to her. "Here."

Glancing up, she took the damp cloth and pressed it to her cheeks. "Thank you. Now if you don't mind…"

He sat down beside her. "So what do you think? Was it the chili fries, the chocolate shake, the jalapeños or maybe—"

"*Stop,*" she said on a groan. "I don't need you to tell me it was stupid. I learned that all by myself, thank you very much."

Smiling, he took her chin in his hand and lifted her face. Her skin looked like chalk. "You need to learn to pace yourself, Clair, that's all. Maybe inch out into the cold water, instead of just jumping in. Walk before you run."

"I've been inching and walking my entire life, Jacob," she said softly. "I don't care if the water is cold, I don't care if I fall. I've already missed out on so much. I'll make mistakes, but whatever they are, they'll be mine."

"So the life of a pampered princess is not all it's cracked up to be, is it?" he asked, cocking his head.

"I won't make excuses for who I am, or how I was

raised," she said defensively, then closed her eyes and exhaled slowly. "Or who I thought I was anyway."

He'd been around spoiled, wealthy women who thought the world should revolve around them. But there was something different about Clair. An innocence that unnerved him, made him want to get in his car and drive away as fast and as far as he could.

For a moment, he considered doing just that, then swore silently and scooped her up in his arms instead. She gasped, then stiffened at his unexpected maneuver.

"Well, Miss Beauchamp," he said evenly, "since you don't want to 'miss out' on anything, I suggest we get you in bed."

Her eyes popped open wide. "I never said, I mean, I certainly wasn't implying that I wanted to, I mean, that we should—"

He carried her to the bed. "Relax, Clair. I meant to *sleep*. We've got a long couple of days ahead of us before we get to Wolf River. But hey—" he dropped her on the squeaky mattress "—thanks for thinking of me."

Her cheeks turned scarlet against her still pale skin. "Oh," she said somewhere between a croak and a squeak.

She looked so lost lying on the bed, so…disappointed?…that Jacob considered "jumping in" himself. He stared at her, saw the outline of her soft breasts against his white T-shirt, the faint press of hardened nipples, that long expanse of legs covered by his sweatpants. A jolt of lust shot through his blood.

"Get some sleep," he said through the dryness in

his throat as he turned. "We'll hit the road around nine."

He walked through the connecting door to their rooms, closed it tightly behind him, then groaned.

This, he thought miserably, was going to be one long trip.

It was dark when Jacob woke. He wasn't even certain why he *had* awakened, especially considering it was—he slitted a glance at the red dial of the nightstand clock—*5:46 a.m.*? Good God, it was still the middle of the night.

And was that coffee he smelled? He breathed in the wonderful scent and nestled his head back into his pillow. He'd have to get himself a cup when he finally did wake up in a couple of hours.

But there was another smell, he realized dimly. A light, fresh scent of...peaches? Where was that coming from?

He heard her whisper his name at the same time he felt the mattress dip on the other side of the bed. When he bolted upright, muttering a swear word, she gasped.

"What's wrong?" He could see her outline in the early dawn seeping through the closed drapes, but he couldn't make out her face. She'd already jumped up from the edge of the bed and stood a safe distance away, holding a mug of coffee in her hands. "What's happened?"

"Nothing's happened." Her voice broke, and she cleared her throat. "I wanted to talk to you."

"At five forty-six in the morning?" he hissed.

"It couldn't wait."

"The hell it can't." He pulled the covers up and turned his back to her.

"I have a plan." She came around the bed, flipped on the bedside lamp, then set the steaming mug of coffee on the nightstand.

He winced at the stream of light, was almost enticed by the coffee, then shook it off and growled, "Go away, Clair, or I won't be responsible for anything that happens."

Folding her arms, she looked down her nose at him. "What's *that* supposed to mean?"

He rose on one elbow, let the covers slide down his bare chest and narrowed a look at her. Her hair, still damp from the shower she'd obviously just taken, curved around her pretty oval face and touched the top of the sleeveless button-up pink blouse she wore. She'd pulled on slim-fitting black capris that showed off her long legs and narrow hips. Her feet were bare, her toenails painted with pink glitter polish.

Dammit. He wanted to consume her whole. He fisted the covers in his hands to keep himself from dragging her into his bed and *showing* her *exactly* what he meant.

But he wouldn't. Not only was she a client, she was trouble. With a capital *T.* Clair Beauchamp was complicated. He preferred simple when it came to sex and women.

"Wasn't going into naked, strange men's motel rooms on your mother's forbidden list?" he snarled.

He saw her hesitation, then she squared her shoulders. "Well, that's partly what I want to talk to you about."

Once again she'd caught him off balance. Another reason to keep his distance from this woman. "You want to talk to me about strange, naked men in hotel rooms?''

"Of course not." She rolled her eyes. "I want to talk to you about my plan."

On a groan, he slid back under the covers. "Have you always been this big a pest?"

"That's the point, Jacob." She sank down on the floor and sat on her heels. "I've never been a pest. My entire life I've always been expected to, and always have, behaved in a certain manner. It never occurred to me there was an option."

"You're telling me you never rebelled, even when you were a teenager?" Even for a socialite priss like Clair, that was hard to believe. He thought about all the foster homes he'd been through, the hell he'd raised through his most difficult years. "*Every* kid drives their parents nuts at least once."

"I gave the term PC a whole new meaning." She stared down at her clasped hands. "For me it was Perfect Child. More than anything, I wanted my parents' approval."

"Not an easy job, I gather," he said.

She looked up sharply, a snap of fire in her blue eyes. "I wasn't the poor little rich girl, if that's what you're thinking. My parents have always been wonderful to me. Have always done what they thought was best for me. They were protective, yes, overly, yes, but only because they loved me. And because I loved them, I wanted to please them."

At the cost of pleasing herself, Jacob realized. It didn't take a shrink to figure out she'd lost one family and was afraid she'd lose another if she wasn't—in her mind's eye—the "Perfect Child." Even though she'd only been two when her birth parents had died, the memory was locked in her little brain and stayed with her.

But this was hardly the time for Psych 101.

On a sigh, he sat and dragged both hands through his hair. "So what's your plan?"

Smiling, she picked up the coffee mug and handed it to him. "My plan is no plan."

"Excuse me?"

"I've had my whole life mapped out for me, like a paint-by-number. For just a little while, I want to be spontaneous. Impulsive. Irresponsible."

Bad idea, he thought, but who was he to tell her what to do? She'd had enough of that in her life already. He took a sip of coffee. "Fine. I'll get you to Wolf River and you can do and be whatever you want from that point."

"I mean *before* I get to Wolf River. I want to take the long way there. See things I've never seen. Do things I've never done. Experience as much as I can along the way." Her eyes were as bright as her smile. "And I want you to drive me."

"Me?" Coffee sloshed over the sides of his cup. *Very* bad idea. "No way."

"Jacob, I'll pay you for your time." She rocked forward off her heels and laid her arms on the edge of the bed. "What's another three or four days?"

The heat of her body and the scent of peaches drifting off her smooth skin sent his blood racing. Could she possibly be so oblivious not to realize the effect she had on him? Or was she manipulating him to get what she wanted?

Either way, he felt the slow rise of anger. He set the coffee mug down, then startled her when he took hold of her shoulders and brought her close.

"Let me spell it out for you, Clair," he said narrowing his gaze. "Client or no client, I don't trust myself to keep my hands off you for the next two days, let alone another three or four."

She stared at him, her eyes wide. "I trust you," she said quietly.

He didn't *want* her to trust him, dammit. Didn't want that kind of responsibility.

"You want spontaneity? You want impulsive?" he said through gritted teeth. "Fine. You got it."

He dragged her closer and covered her mouth with his, felt the shock wave course through her body. He was shocked, as well, not only at the raw intensity of his own need, but the fact she didn't pull away. He parted those incredible lips of hers with his tongue, then dived inside.

And still she didn't pull away.

She was every bit as sweet as he'd imagined. He tipped her head back and deepened the kiss even more, felt her shiver of response and her low, soft moan. Her lips molded to his, then tentatively she met his tongue with her own.

It was the shimmer of innocence that had him yanking his head back. He stared down at her, watched her thick lashes slowly rise. There was confusion in her eyes, and desire. Definitely desire. Her lips were still parted and wet from his kiss.

He'd expected her to slap him, or at the very least, to tell him off. The fact that she did neither nearly had him dragging her back to him again.

He wanted to, dammit. His body ached to bring her to his bed.

But he wouldn't. Somehow, somewhere, he knew there'd be a price he wasn't willing to pay.

"Don't trust me," he said dryly and released her so suddenly she fell back on the floor. "Get yourself another man."

She sat there staring at him, then slowly, as unexpected as everything else was with this woman, she started to laugh.

"What's so damn funny?"

"Whatever on earth made you think I'm looking for a man?" she said, crossing her arms over her stomach. "Good heavens, the *last* thing I need or want right now is a man."

"Is that so?"

"Don't take offense, Jacob." Tucking her hair back behind her ears, she sat down on her heels again. "I mean, that kiss was very nice and all, but I assure you I wasn't looking for anything more than a ride to Wolf River with a few detours along the way."

His kiss was *very nice?* He frowned darkly. He'd show her *very nice...*

But she was already up on her feet and moving toward the door. "I'm sorry you don't want the job," she said over her shoulder. "I'll send you a check for your time and expenses. Thank you for everything you've done for me and if you—"

"Just stop right there."

She paused at the connecting door and looked back at him. "Yes?"

"What do you think you're doing?"

"I'm going to pack, then call a rental car company to come pick me up."

"You're going to drive yourself?" he asked incredulously.

She turned and lifted a brow. "I don't believe that's any of your business."

"Well, I'm making it my business, dammit." He grabbed the sheets, then wrapped them around him as he slid off the bed.

Damn fool woman.

Her eyes widened when he stomped across the room toward her. "We'll leave in fifteen minutes and you better be ready. Until I've had at least three cups of coffee, don't speak to me. Got that?"

"All right," she said demurely.

"Now unless you want an eyeful," he snapped, "I suggest you get the hell out of my room."

She moved quickly across the threshold, then shut the door tightly behind her. Jacob stared at the closed door for a full minute and wondered what the hell had just happened.

You lost your mind, Carver, he said, swearing hotly. *That's what happened.*

The No-Plan, Plan, my ass.

Still swearing, he headed for the shower and decided it was going to be a cold one.

Four

Clair suspected that Jacob kept the volume on his CD player high to deter conversation from her as much to enjoy the music. She didn't mind, not only because she enjoyed the diverse selection of rock he played—Dave Matthews, Beatles, Stones, Springsteen, Zeppelin—but because she needed a little time alone with her own thoughts at the moment, as well.

She glanced at Jacob, watched his thumbs move to the beat of ''Jumpin' Jack Flash,'' and wondered if he knew he hummed along with most of the songs and even occasionally, under his breath, sang a line or chorus. But then he'd catch himself and sink back into that brooding silence of his. It was obvious he was used to being alone in this big car, and he wasn't happy about anyone invading the sanctity of his space.

They'd left Lenore three hours ago and at her request, stopped for bottled water in a town called Don't Blink, then crossed the state line into Georgia. The day was hot and humid, and Clair was thankful that Jacob's car had an air conditioner powerful enough to keep a penguin cool.

Or a woman whose body was still on fire after being thoroughly and completely kissed.

Jacob's kiss had sizzled her brain and scorched her body clear down to her toes. Even now, her lips still tingled and her stomach fluttered. Her entire life, Clair had been taught how to behave with poise and grace. To be calm and composed in every situation. One kiss from Jacob, and she'd nearly melted into the floor.

She'd nearly begged for more.

Oliver's kisses had been…polite compared to Jacob. Pleasant. Controlled. Tepid. Jacob's kiss had been wild and reckless. *Hot.*

He'd told her he didn't think he could keep his hands off her, and though his words had made her heart skip and her breath stop, she didn't believe him. A man like Jacob couldn't really be interested in an inexperienced, bluenose stiff like herself. She knew he'd only said that, then kissed her to intimidate her, to change her mind about taking detours on the way to Wolf River.

But his intentions had not made the kiss any less thrilling. If anything, he'd proven to her that there was a whole world waiting to explore, to experience. And while she might not be ready for the Jacob Carvers of the world, she was definitely ready for a little excitement, a little adventure.

While she pretended to be engrossed in the lush greenery of the passing farms and hillsides along the highway, she cast a sideways glance at him. The black T-shirt he had on fit snugly over his broad chest and muscular arms. He wore a day-old beard and a pair of sunglasses. A small, jagged scar over his right eyebrow reminded her of a bolt of lightning. His jaw was strong, his nose slightly crooked, his mouth—her breath caught just thinking about his mouth—was bracketed by lines on either side.

Even though *she* wasn't looking for a man at the moment, she could only imagine that Jacob had more than his share of interested females. The man exuded the kind of raw masculinity that would have women dropping at his feet.

She yanked her gaze away, disgusted at her line of thinking. In a meadow beyond a white rail fence, she saw two little boys running through knee-high grass, pulling red and yellow kites high in the air behind them. Long, blue streamers swirled from the bottom of each kite.

"I've never done that," she said absently, watching the kites dip and soar with the air current.

He lowered the music. "What?"

She turned in her seat, still staring out the window as the car passed the meadow. "I've never flown a kite."

"Never?"

She felt silly now that she'd said it. Leaning back in her seat, she looked over at Jacob. "Have you?"

"Of course."

"What color was it?"

He furrowed his brow. "Color?"

"Your kite."

"Oh. Orange, with the number O1."

"Why, 01?"

He looked at her as if she knew nothing. "The General Lee."

"General Lee?"

"You know. *The Dukes of Hazard.* Bo Duke, Luke Duke, Daisy Duke."

"The TV show." Understanding finally dawned. "I've heard of it."

"But you've never seen it?" he said in disbelief. "Jeez, you *did* lead a sheltered life."

"More like a scheduled life." She thought of all the after school lessons, the Saturday recitals. "Ballet, piano, Cotillion."

"Cotillion?"

"Formal dances for young people," she explained.

Jacob shuddered. "I'd rather drive nails through my toes."

She laughed. "Sometimes it felt like that if you got the wrong partner. But we learned proper etiquette and social graces."

"Yeah? Like what?"

She sat very straight and lifted her chin. "Introductions, for one. 'Mr. Carver,'" she said in a very stuffy voice. "'May I introduce you to Mrs. Widebottom. Mrs. Widebottom, Mr. Carver.'"

He tilted his head down and glanced at her over the top of his sunglasses. "You're kidding, right?"

"Absolutely not. Then, Mr. Carver, you would ask Mrs. Widebottom if she would like a glass of punch. 'Why, yes, Mr. Carver, I'd love a glass of punch.'" Clair batted her eyes. "After you fill the punch glass for her, you then ask if she'd like a cookie. Once you have punch and cookies, you have a conversation."

"You mean you can't just eat the cookies?"

"Heavens, no. You have to talk first. Engaging

your partner in polite conversation is required. 'Mr. Carver, that's a very nice T-shirt you're wearing. Is it Tommy Hillfiger, by chance?''

One corner of his mouth lifted. '''Why, no, Mrs. Widebottom, it's Sidewalk Sam.'''

'''I'm not familiar with that designer,''' Clair said with a sniff. '''New York, or Paris?'''

'''Lower East Side. Sam's on his corner from noon to six every afternoon. Three shirts for twelve bucks, but if you tell him you know me, he'll cut you a deal.'''

It was the first time Jacob had truly heard Clair laugh, and the sound rippled over his skin. The smile on her lips faded when she turned back to the window and stared out.

"Did you ever wonder," she said thoughtfully, "what your life would be like if your mother had never left?"

He had from time to time. But he knew what she was really wondering about was how different her own life would be if her birth mother hadn't died. He shrugged, then focused his gaze back on the highway. "You can't change your life. It is what it is."

She shook her head. "It's not that I want to change it, I just want to make it better."

"You already did that yesterday, when you walked out of that church. That took guts, Clair."

"I hurt a lot of people," she said quietly.

"And if you'd married Oliver?" Jacob shifted gears, then changed lanes and passed a ten-wheeler. "Who would you have hurt?"

She turned back from the window. "Me."

"Damn straight." He smiled at her, noticed a sign along the road announcing Ambiance, population two thousand, three hundred and forty-six. Five miles ahead. The next sign was a twenty-foot billboard advertising Doug's Delicious Dogs.

He glanced over at her, saw her staring at the billboard.

"Ms. Beauchamp," he said ever so politely. "May I interest you in a Doug's Delicious Dog?"

Smiling, she looked at him and dipped a hand to her chest. "Why, thank you, Mr. Carver." She laid the Southern drawl on heavy. "If it's not too much trouble, I would adore one."

They pulled into the town of Plug Nickel around seven-thirty that evening. While Jacob checked them into The Night Owl Motel, Clair stretched her legs in the parking lot. Though she'd ridden in airplanes for long periods of time, she'd never traveled or taken vacations by car. Her mother had thought a car too confining and uncomfortable for trips.

Clair loved it. She loved the feel of speed on the open highway, the power of the big car's engine, the passing and ever-changing scenery. She ran her hand over the smooth paint of the shiny black car. Maybe she'd buy one of these vintage cars herself. Nothing this large, of course. Something more compact and sporty. A Mustang or a Corvette.

Definitely a convertible.

Drawn by the country-western music drifting from the restaurant next door to the motel, Clair wandered across the weed-spotted parking lot. A yellow neon sign over the front entrance blinked Weber's Bar and Grill. Arms wrapped around each other, a young couple came out, bringing the scent of barbecue and cigarette smoke with them.

Clair looked back at the motel office; through the glass front window she could see Jacob still waiting at the counter. The clerk had not yet appeared, and even from this distance, Clair could see the tug of annoyance on Jacob's face.

A black, dusty pickup drove by and a wolf whistle pierced the hot evening air. Clair stiffened indignantly, prepared to icily ignore the gauche behavior, when she realized she hadn't been the object of attention. A platinum-blond in a short, black leather skirt, red halter top and black stiletto heels had appeared from the convenience store next door. The woman was probably around Clair's age, though it was hard to tell under the heavy makeup. The blonde lifted a haughty brow as she passed, adjusted the V of her top to increase her already bulging bustline, then went into the restaurant.

Fascinating.

Clair had never been in a place like this before, had never even been *close* to a place like this. She was dying to see what it looked like inside. She looked down at what she was wearing, the black capris, pink tank top and flip-flop sandals, and thought she should probably change into more appropriate clothes, but she didn't have any clothes like the blonde. Besides, she only wanted a peek. She glanced back over her shoulder at Jacob, saw him pacing the motel office.

She'd just pop inside for a minute, she told herself, look around, then pop back out again.

The interior was blissfully air-conditioned, though extremely dark, lit only by the colorful neon beer signs on the walls. Clair waited a moment for her eyes to adjust to the dim light. Sawdust and peanut shells littered the concrete floor. People, mostly young, crowded the bar to the left and filled the pine tables in the center of the room. Between the din of conversation, a baseball game on a television over the bar and a jukebox blasting out a country song about a girl named Norma Jean Riley, it was nearly impossible to hear. Cigarettes were lit at the bar, but where the food was being served, it appeared to be smoke-free. The tangy scent of barbecue sauce hung heavy in the air, reminding Clair she hadn't eaten since they'd stopped in Ambiance for hot dogs.

No one at the tables seemed to notice her, but several heads, male and female, swiveled from the bar area and stared. *Time to go,* she decided. She turned and ran smack dab into a tall, dark-haired man entering the bar.

"Whoa." He put his hands on her shoulders to steady her.

"Pardon me." She attempted to step out of his hold, but he held on and grinned at her.

"What's your hurry, beautiful?" he asked in a voice that sounded like he had rocks in his throat. His white T-shirt said Mad Dog Construction.

He was a nice-looking man, Clair thought, but she didn't care for his hands on her. "I'm terribly sorry. If you'll excuse me, I was just leaving."

"I'll accept your apology if you come have a drink with me."

"Thank you." She smiled cooly, attempted unsuccessfully to slip from his firm grasp. "But I'm afraid I already have plans."

"You can be a little late," he coaxed, still holding her. "It's healthy to keep a guy waiting once in a while."

"Not healthy for you," a deep voice said from behind them.

Mad Dog dropped his hands from Clair and turned around to face Jacob. "Hey, sorry, man." The construction worker shrugged. "Can't blame a guy for trying."

Jacob moved beside Clair and took her arm. "Try somewhere else."

"Sure," the other man said, though he couldn't resist one last look at Clair as he moved past her.

Clair released the breath she'd been holding and looked up at Jacob. "Thank heavens you—"

"Are you crazy?" He hauled her up against him. "What the hell were you thinking, coming into a place like this by yourself?"

"What's wrong with this—"

"Obviously you weren't thinking," he snapped. "God knows what would have happened if I hadn't looked up and seen you sneak in here."

"I didn't sneak in anywhere." She pressed a hand against his rock-hard chest and pushed. She might as well have shoved at a brick wall. "And nothing would have happened. That man was perfectly nice."

Jacob frowned at her. "You call a strange man putting his hands on you 'perfectly nice?'"

"I wasn't watching where I was going and I ran into him." She narrowed her eyes. "And *you* have your hands on me, in case you didn't notice."

Oh, he noticed all right. A twitch jumped in the corner of his left eye. It had been a long day cooped up in the car with Clair. A long day forcing himself to concentrate on the curves of the road instead of the curves of the sweet-smelling woman sitting beside him. A long day keeping his hands on the steering wheel instead of where he really wanted them, which was all over Clair.

He let loose of her, then started to turn. "Let's get out of here."

"I want to stay."

He froze, then swung back around. "What?"

"We're already here." She folded her arms and lifted her chin. "The food here looks and smells wonderful. Give me one good reason we shouldn't eat here."

He could have given her at least ten reasons, all of them sitting at the bar checking her out. He knew if he'd been sitting at the bar, he'd be checking her out, too.

When he'd walked in and seen that guy with his hands on Clair, Jacob had come much too close to punching him out, which could have turned ugly, considering "Mad Dog" obviously had a pack of buddies at the bar, and they probably would have felt it necessary to intervene on their friend's behalf.

Fortunately for everyone, the construction worker appeared to be more of a lover than a fighter and had backed off.

"There's a coffee shop down the street," he said tightly. "It's quieter and—"

"Table for two?" A petite brunette holding menus bounced up and had to yell to be heard over a song about beer and bones.

Clair nodded at the waitress, then followed her through the crowded restaurant to a table in the center of the room.

Damn this woman. Grinding his teeth, crunching peanut shells under his boots, Jacob strode after her.

"Tri-tip and baby back combo is the special tonight." The waitress laid the menus on the table. "What can I get you to drink?"

Jacob dropped down in his chair. "Black and Tan and a cola."

Clair sat primly. "*Two* Black and Tans, please."

He frowned at her when the waitress left. "Do you even know what a Black and Tan is?"

She picked up the menu. "No, but I hope it's cold. I'm very thirsty."

Jacob sighed and prayed for patience.

They ordered two specials when the waitress returned with their drinks and a complimentary basket of deep-fried cheese balls. Jacob settled back in his chair and watched Clair delicately pick up her glass, then lift it cheerfully toward him. He raised his to her, as well.

She took a big sip, then froze, an expression of utter disgust on her face.

"Sometimes you have to chew it a little to help it down." He smiled and took a gulp of his own dark, thick beer. "You'll get used to the taste after a few sips."

She pressed her lips into a thin line, then closed her eyes as she swallowed.

If only he'd had a camera.

Enjoying himself now, Jacob glanced around the restaurant. For a Monday night, the place seemed unusually crowded, but he supposed there wasn't much else to do in Plug Nickel. At the far back of the restaurant, two pool tables had games going, and in the front of the room, a bald-headed deejay was setting up his equipment on a small stage.

The waitress placed two heaping plates of food on the table while a bus boy delivered two glasses of ice

water, then nearly spilled it he was so busy staring at
Clair. When Clair smiled at the smitten pup and
thanked him, he grinned awkwardly, then tripped over
his own feet backing away. Too busy washing away
the taste of the beer, Clair didn't notice.

Was she really that oblivious to her effect on men?
Jacob wondered. He realized she'd lived in a confined
community of culture and privilege, that her life had
been arranged right down to the man she would
marry, but still, how could she be so unaware of her
looks? He knew from his report that her birth father
was Cherokee, her mother Welsh. The combination
had created an exotic appearance, a dark sensuality
that could make a monk forget his vows.

He watched her take another sip of her beer, shudder, then dig delicately into her food. An expression
of sheer pleasure, something that bordered on sexual,
washed over her face as she chewed. The bite of tri-
tip Jacob had taken turned to cardboard, and his throat
went dry. The blood from his brain went south.

The woman had to be playing him for a fool, dammit. She *couldn't* be as innocent as she appeared.

He kept his eyes and attention on his food, determined not to let her get to him. When the deejay
announced it was karaoke night, Jacob was happy for
the distraction, even though the first volunteer who
sang Wynonna Judd's "Why Not Me?" had a voice
like a slipping radiator belt. Fascination lit Clair's big
blue eyes as she watched the different singers belt out
an assortment of country and pop tunes.

"You should try it," she yelled over the music.
"You have a nice voice."

He gave her a look that said, *not in a million years.*
Smiling, she pushed her plate aside and stood. He

thought for a moment she was going to go up and sing, but she excused herself and headed for the ladies' room. He watched the sway of her hips as she made her way through the crowded room, frowned when he noticed that several other men were watching her, as well.

He stabbed a bite of meat. What the hell did he care if other guys stared at her? It wasn't like he was *with* her, or they were on a date or anything. Hell, even on those rare occasions when he'd been dating a woman on a regular basis, he'd never gotten himself worked up if another man looked. So why should it matter with Clair?

It didn't matter. Not at all.

He watched a man sing his own rendition of Garth Brooks ''Friends in Low Places,'' then a woman who did a pretty good job with an old Patsy Cline song. He'd finished his meal, a second beer and still no sign of Clair. He told himself he wasn't worried, he was simply annoyed. Extremely annoyed.

Frowning, he paid the bill, then headed in the direction of the ladies' room. Honest to God, he was going to have Lojack installed in the woman.

He relaxed a little when he found her standing with another woman, watching a pool game between Mad Dog and one of his buddies. Based on the amount of cheers and whistles, there was some heavy betting going on.

Clair's companion, a blonde in a short leather skirt, red halter top and high heels you could pick ice with, was busy talking and gesturing toward the pool table while Clair listened intently. When Jacob came up behind them, the blonde saw him first. She was dressed to catch a man's eye, exposing more skin than fabric. He returned the smile she threw him, though more out of habit than interest. She was a fine-looking woman, but standing next to Clair, the blonde paled.

He slipped an easy arm around Clair's shoulders, as much to lead her away as to establish who was with whom. Somehow he doubted that Clair's Cotillion lessons had included singles bars and lounge lizards. He felt her stiffen, then saw the indignation in her narrowed eyes when she turned to see who had dared manhandle her. She frowned at him, but did not step away.

"Jacob," Clair said over the noise, "this is Mindy Moreland. Mindy, Jacob Carver."

Jacob nodded; Mindy lifted her beer glass to him and smiled wider.

"Mindy is head of housekeeping at The Night Owl," Clair said as if it were the most fascinating job on earth. "We met in the rest room and I told her we're staying there."

Loud groans and cat calls drew their attention back to the pool game which had just ended with Mad Dog as the victor. Mindy ran over to throw her arms around the construction worker, and the loser ordered pitchers of beer for everyone. From the opposite end of the restaurant, a man was struggling through Roy Orbison's "Pretty Woman."

Jacob had to get out of here. Now.

Tightening his hold on Clair, he leaned down and whispered in her ear, "Let's go."

"You go ahead."

He stared at her blankly. "What?"

"I'm going to hang around a little." She waved a hand, as if to dismiss him. "I'll see you in the morning."

I'll see you in the morning?

Like *hell.*

"Dammit, Clair," he said tightly, "this isn't the kind of place a nice girl hangs around alone."

"Mindy's nice, and she's alone. We're going to play a game of pool."

Jacob looked at Mindy, watched her give Mad Dog a big, wet kiss. Mindy was an *exceptionally* nice girl, he thought, but knew better than to give Clair his opinion of the woman.

"Fine," he said through clenched teeth. "*I'll* play you a game of pool. If I win, we leave."

"All right. But if I win—" she hesitated, thought carefully, then smiled "—you have to sing. And I pick the song."

Like *that* would ever happen. "Absolutely not."

She arched a brow. "So you think I'll beat you?"

He heard the challenge in her voice and knew he should walk out. Just leave her. It was no skin off his nose if she wanted to hang out in a bar and play pool. She was a big girl, for God sakes. Isn't that how she'd learn? By making mistakes?

But he couldn't do it. He felt a…responsibility. Her brothers had paid him to find her, Clair was paying him to bring her to Wolf River. He had an obligation to see she got there safe and sound.

And besides, he'd never turned down a challenge in his life. He put his nose to hers. They'd be out of here in ten minutes tops.

"You're on."

They snagged a table and two pool cues, then Mindy, excited over the game, racked the balls. Jacob considered offering the break to Clair, maybe even setting her up for a shot or two.

Then he watched Mad Dog come over to wish her luck, and Jacob felt his lip curl.

No mercy.

"Lag for break," he barked. When Clair stared at him in confusion, Mindy explained the term. Whoever banked off the far end of the pool table and came closest to the opposite cushion took the break.

Jacob took his shot, grinned confidently when he came with three inches. Clair took her shot and came within two.

Luck, he thought, but wasn't worried. She'd need more than luck to win the game. When she leaned over and wiggled her hips to get in position, it was all Jacob could do to keep his mind on the game and his eye on the table.

When Clair broke and sank three balls, two solids and a stripe, he narrowed a gaze at her.

Damn lucky.

"What do I do now?" Clair asked her new best-buddy Mindy.

"Pick solids or stripes," the blonde said.

To Jacob's annoyance, a crowd had gathered around. When Clair chose stripes, clearly giving him the advantage, he scowled at her.

In perfect form, she sank the fourteen ball, then the twelve.

Sweat broke out on his brow when she sank the nine ball.

Nobody was *that* lucky. Son of a *bitch.* He set his jaw so tight he could have cracked a molar.

Little Miss Innocent had set him up.

He got a break on the next shot when the sound of shattering glass from the bar distracted her. No fool, he made every shot count. He sank four balls, then just missed the one ball on a double bank. He'd pick it up next turn.

He never got the chance.

He watched in disbelief as one after the other, she sank her remaining balls, then smoothly popped in the eight ball.

She'd beat him. She'd actually *won*.

There were cheers and whistles around the table. Mindy hugged Clair and Mad Dog gave her a high-five. Jacob stared at the surreal scene, then leveled a gaze at her. "You've played pool before."

She shook her head. "Only snooker with my father. He's very good."

Very good? Jacob lifted a brow.

Clair handed her cue to Mindy, then came around the table. "You aren't going to welch on our bet, are you?"

He set his teeth. "Let's just get this over with."

Clair supposed she could let Jacob off the hook. In a way, she *had* hustled him. She'd played snooker since she was a child and was better than good at it. Though the rules and strategy were completely different from standard pool, the basics of how to strike a ball were the same. She also knew that because he hadn't expected her to beat him, she'd caught him off guard and he hadn't played to his ability.

It hardly seemed fair or proper to compel him to make good on their bet, she thought. After all, wasn't it enough she'd actually won? Shouldn't she be the gracious victor and allow him a little dignity?

She glanced at his scowling face.

Nah.

Slipping her arm through his, she dragged him up to the deejay.

He glared at her while she scanned the list of songs. Dylan, Sinatra, Manilow—he'd *hate* that one—Morrison, Stewart…

Bingo.

She made her selection and handed it to him, then hurried off to find a seat before he could grab her by the throat. To Clair's pleasure and Jacob's disgust, it seemed that every person in the place had gathered around to watch.

The music started. Jacob gulped down a swallow of beer Mad Dog offered him from his front row seat, then handed it back and stepped to the microphone.

When he yanked down a lock of dark hair from the center of his forehead, narrowed his eyes and swiveled his hips, the women went wild.

"Love me tender…"

Five

Clair woke the next morning to the sound of "Jailhouse Rock" playing in her head. After "Love Me Tender," the crowd had insisted on another Elvis tune. Jacob had done his best to refuse, but he'd been outnumbered. If he hadn't sang another song, the women might not have let him out alive.

Every woman in the place had melted when he'd sang the first song, then screamed when he'd sang the next. By the end of "Jailhouse Rock," he'd had everyone in the entire restaurant and bar up on their feet, singing and dancing along.

Jacob Carver was quite a package. Not only of surprises, but of contradictions, as well.

He'd made it clear to her that he wasn't her baby-sitter, yet he'd stood guard over her last night from the moment he'd found her in the bar with David—or Mad Dog, as Jacob called him. She'd seen him narrowing that dark gaze of his at any male who looked at her in a way he didn't like. Clair wasn't certain if she was annoyed or relieved that the men had kept their distance. Probably a little of both. Fund-raisers and ladies' luncheons had not exactly prepared her for the wild and raucous beer-drinking singles crowd.

Still, she couldn't remember when she'd ever laughed so hard, or when she'd had so much fun. Just thinking about it now made her smile. She'd been relaxed. No social niceties to worry about, no restraints.

Her smile faded. And still she hadn't felt as if she'd fit in. Not there.

Not anywhere.

All the ballet, the dance, the Ivy League schools. The charity balls and formal dinners, the afternoon teas. She'd never felt as if she completely belonged. She'd never felt as if she were a part of the whole.

It certainly wasn't for lack of love. Her parents loved her deeply, and she loved them, too.

But something had always been missing. Something she couldn't put a finger on. Something as elusive as a scent carried on a breeze, or a dream she couldn't remember.

She'd taken child development in college. She understood that all memories from childhood, even the actual process of being born, were retained and stored in the brain. Feelings, textures, smells, images. Everything was there. Nothing truly forgotten.

With a sigh, she stared at the acoustic ceiling over her head. She'd spent the first two years of her life with a different family. Mother, father, two brothers.

A different house, yard, environment. She wanted to remember *something*. Even *one* little thing.

She squeezed her eyes shut, took a slow, deep breath and let her mind drift.

Pink clouds floated by…smiling blue eyes, eyes so like her own. Clair felt the warmth of the woman's arms around her. They were outside…so many people, laughing and talking. Two little boys ran in circles around her…

The image melted away, too, and though she tried, Clair could not pull it back up.

Was that her family? Had she simply invoked the images because she wanted so badly to remember even one little thing from her past? Or had they been real?

Her heart beat faster at the thought. Her hands shook as she dragged on a short cotton robe, then flew out of bed.

When Jacob heard Clair knocking at the connecting door, he groaned and pulled his pillow over his head. The woman woke up too damn early.

"Go away," he shouted.

He heard the sound of the door opening and burrowed deeper into his bed. "So help me, woman—"

"Jacob, I'm sorry." Her voice bounced with excitement. "I just have to tell someone."

"Go tell the janitor," he growled. "He was banging on the air conditioner outside my door a minute ago. I'm sure he'd be more than happy to hear about how you hustled me last night."

She dropped down on her knees beside the bed. "I let you win the second game, didn't I?"

"*Let* me win?" He popped his head out from under

the pillow. "The hell you say. I beat your butt fair and square."

"Okay," she said affably, which only aggravated him all the more. "But that's not what I want to talk about. I remembered something."

"You woke me up to tell me you *remembered* something?" He fisted his hands in his pillow, rather than her pretty little neck, then did his best to think about how easy it would be to drag her into his bed with him and relieve the ever-growing tension in his body. "You know, for a woman who's supposed to be so well-mannered, that's damn rude."

"It's about my family." Though still heavy from sleep, her eyes sparkled in the early morning light. "My birth family."

"Your birth family?" He furrowed his brow, rose up on one elbow. "You remembered something from when you were two years old?"

"Just a fragment," she said breathlessly. "A fleeting image."

He sat, dragged a hand through his hair. "Clair, considering everything, it would be easy for your imagination to—"

"It *wasn't* my imagination," she insisted. "I know it sounds strange, but we were outside with lots of other people, there were pink clouds, a woman with eyes like mine, two little boys. It was *real,* Jacob. I know it was."

Pink clouds?

Interesting.

Though Jacob knew quite a bit about little Elizabeth Blackhawk and her family, he'd been asked not to tell Clair any more than necessary. Her brothers had decided they wanted to give her details and share their memories with her.

But he felt she needed to know about this. That it was important for her to know.

"You were at a county fair with your family the day of the accident." Her gaze met his. "They sell cotton candy at fairs."

"Pink clouds," she whispered, then dropped her forehead down on the edge of the bed. "My brothers," she said raggedly. "Rand and Seth?"

"What about them?"

"Were their names changed, too?"

"Since they were older when they were adopted, only their last names are different. Instead of Blackhawk, it's Rand Sloan and Seth Granger."

"Blackhawk," she murmured the name, then lifted her head. "It's so familiar. It feels—" she put a hand to her heart "—so right."

He watched her blink furiously at the sudden tears in her eyes and look away.

"Hey." He took her chin in his hand and turned her face back toward him. "What's this for?"

"I—" Swallowing hard, she whispered, "Jacob, what if they don't like me?"

"What are you talking about?"

She wiped at a tear that slid from the corner of her eye. "What if I don't fit in with them? What if after they meet me, I'm not the sister they remember?"

Who the hell cares? he wanted to say, but he realized that she did. Very much. Something shifted in his chest as he stared at her, something completely foreign to him. He didn't like it one little bit.

He had a sudden, fierce urge to take her to his bed, to make nothing else in her world matter. Sex could

do that. Make a person forget everything, if only for
a little while. They would both find pleasure there, he
knew. Just looking at her, with that tousled hair and
those liquid eyes made his blood boil. The thought of
her long legs wrapped around him, imagining what it
would feel like to bury himself deep inside her, made
him instantly hard.

Grating his teeth, he held back the threatening
groan. He'd never taken advantage of a woman's vul-
nerability before. And dammit, he sure as hell didn't
plan to start now.

With something between a sigh and a swear word,
he reached for her. She stiffened at his touch, but he
tugged insistently until she sat on the bed beside him.

"Relax, Clair." He pulled her into his arms. "I'm
not going to jump your bones."

"I've heard *that* one before." But she did lay her
head on his chest. "Usually a minute or two before,
'I just want to hold you.'"

Jacob smiled, remembered using that line a time or
two in high school. "I *am* just going to hold you. If
I was intending to do more, you'd know."

"I would?" she said quietly.

"If I was doing it right, you would."

Chuckling softly, she relaxed against him. "I know
I'm being silly, worrying if Rand and Seth will like
me, if they will want me to be a part of their lives.
It's just that I've always wanted a sister or a brother."

"Maybe you should worry if you'll like them,"
Jacob told her, tucking a strand of hair behind her
ear.

"Maybe."

The warm breath of her sigh whispered over his

chest, and when she slid her hand up his arm, Jacob felt his heart slam against his ribs.

This was a bad idea, he thought.

Her fingers moved back and forth on his shoulder.

A *really* bad idea.

Her lips lightly brushed his collarbone.

Dammit, dammit, *dammit.*

He knew there were reasons he shouldn't just give in to what they both wanted. Good reasons. But with her touching him like she was, knowing she wasn't wearing much under that little robe, and that he wasn't wearing anything at all, he was having a hell of a time remembering what those reasons were.

And in roughly two seconds, even if he did remember them, he wouldn't give a damn.

Setting his teeth, he took hold of her arms and held her away. "We should get going."

Her eyes, heavy-lidded and filled with the same need he felt burning in his veins, lifted to his. "What?"

"It's late, Clair," he said tightly. "We need to get on the road."

"Oh." She blinked, then her cheeks flushed bright pink. "Of course. I'll just…go get ready."

"Good idea."

She slid off the bed, hesitated, then turned and headed for her room.

"Clair?"

From the doorway, she glanced over her shoulder.

"You didn't really let me win last night, did you?"

She smiled slowly. "Of course not. Like you said, you beat me fair and square."

He frowned at the door she closed behind her, then said loudly, "I *did* beat you, dammit."

He heard her laugh from the other side of the door. Swearing, he tossed the covers off and stomped to the bathroom, wondering what he'd ever done to deserve the likes of Clair Beauchamp.

An hour later, while Jacob checked them out of the motel, Clair stood in the parking lot with Mindy and said goodbye.

Dressed in a simple black skirt, white cotton blouse and plain black flats, The Night Owl's head house-keeper looked like a different woman from the sexpot Clair had met at Weber's Bar and Grill the night before. Clair actually thought Mindy looked more beautiful without the heavy makeup, and younger, too.

"Maybe you can call me after you get to Wolf River," Mindy said after Clair explained briefly why she and Jacob were driving together to Wolf River. "I can't wait to know what happens."

"I'm a little nervous to meet my brothers," Clair admitted, "but excited, too."

Mindy grinned. "I'm not talking about your brothers, though I can't wait to hear about them, too. I'm talking about you and Jacob."

"Me and Jacob?" Clair felt her stomach do a back flip. "There's nothing between us."

"Right." Mindy gave a snort of laughter. "That's why he couldn't take his eyes off you last night, unless it was to warn off every other guy that you were already taken."

"We weren't—aren't—together that way," Clair insisted. "We have a business relationship."

"I don't know if you're trying to convince me or yourself," Mindy said with an arched eyebrow, "but

I know when a man's interested, and trust me, he's definitely interested.''

Clair glanced toward the motel office where Jacob stood at the counter paying the bill. Yesterday, when she hadn't considered him being attracted to her, he'd kissed her and told her he didn't think he could keep his hands off her. Then this morning, when she'd practically thrown herself at him, he'd rejected her.

The man completely confused and frustrated her.

Shaking her head, Clair looked back at Mindy. ''I think he sees me as a responsibility, like a package to be delivered. One that has Fragile stamped all over it.''

''Well, then maybe you need to rewrap that package, honey,'' Mindy drawled. ''Show him you won't break so easy.''

Clair laughed at the idea, watched Jacob come out of the motel office, slip his sunglasses on, then head toward them.

''Damn,'' Mindy muttered as Jacob approached. ''That is one fine man.''

Clair couldn't agree more. His dark, rugged looks and tall muscular build were enough to make a woman's breath catch, but add that dazzling smile along with his easy, confident stride, and the effect was deadly to any female within fifty yards.

''You ready?'' He pulled his keys out of his pocket.

Clair turned to Mindy and gave her a hug while Jacob started his car. The engine roared to life, then rumbled, like a caged beast waiting to be released.

They waved goodbye to Mindy, bought coffee and French toast strips at a fast-food drive-thru, then left the town of Plug Nickel and headed for the Interstate.

"What's your whim today, Miss Beauchamp?" Jacob sipped on his coffee. "You have a town that calls to you?"

Clair dipped her French toast strip in a tiny plastic vat of maple syrup, took a bite, then dragged her map out of the glove box. While she chewed, she studied the crisscross of cities and towns. The names flew at her: Raccoon, Rainbow, Yazoo, Picayune.

Tapping the map, she looked up at Jacob and smiled. "Liberty, Louisiana."

"You got coolant coming out of the water pump. Probably a failed seal." Odell, the gas station mechanic, stared down under the open hood of Jacob's car. "Lucky thing for you the engine didn't overheat."

Frowning, Jacob stood beside the middle-aged mechanic and bit back the swear word on the tip of his tongue. *Lucky* would hardly be the word he would have used. After driving all day, stopping at every little town along the way that caught Clair's attention, they'd been ten minutes out of Liberty when the temperature gauge had started to rise. By the time they'd pulled into town, a cloud of thick steam had begun to seep out from under the hood of the car.

"How long?" Jacob glanced in the direction of the gas station office where Clair had gone in search of a restroom, then looked back at the mechanic.

"Wellll…" Odell stretched the word out. "It's already two, but I can try to pull the pump this afternoon."

Try? Jacob ground his teeth. "And you think it might be done when?"

"Hard to say." Odell scratched the back of his

neck. "Maybe tomorrow. Can't promise, though. Gordon, my helper, went fishing this afternoon. I'm all by myself, and I've got a bad back."

"What if I help you?" Jacob suggested. Clair had spotted several antiques stores she'd wanted to browse through when they'd drove down the main street in the small town. Jacob not only welcomed the opportunity to avoid shopping of any kind, he was nervous about letting anyone work on his car beside himself.

Odell gave Jacob a dubious look. "You know how to reverse directions on a rachet?"

"I restored her myself from the ground up, dropped the drive train in the chassis and added ram air induction."

"426 or 440?"

"426 Hemi."

Odell nodded with approval. "Grab yourself a pair of overalls from the office, son. Just ask Tina."

The afternoon was hot and muggy; the deep blue sky laced with white clouds. The smell of motor oil and warm asphalt hung heavy in the air, but when Jacob opened the glass office door, an icy blast of air-conditioning and the scent of lemon deodorizer rushed out to meet him.

No sign of Clair, but behind the counter of a small convenience store area, a pretty woman probably in her early thirties sat reading a Hollywood entertainment magazine. Everything about her was red. Her short, spiked hair, her lips, her long nails. Even her low-cut, wraparound top was the color of a fire engine.

"Tina?"

She looked up, then slowly slid her gaze over him. "That's me, sugar."

"Odell said I should get a pair of overalls from you."

One hopeful brow shot up. "You working here now?"

"Just helping out for the afternoon."

"Too bad." The clerk laid her elbows on the counter and leaned forward with a provocative smile. "No fair you know my name and I don't know yours."

"Jacob." He would have had to been dead not to notice—and appreciate—the cleavage the redhead seemed determined to show him. "Jacob Carver."

"Tina Holland." She stood, gave her spandex-clad hips an extra swing as she moved to a closet at the back of her cubicle, then glanced over her shoulder and sized him with her eyes. "Large or extra-large?"

When her gaze lingered on his crotch, Jacob shifted awkwardly. "Extra-large."

"Of course you are." Smiling, Tina pulled out a pair of clean overalls and moved back toward him. "So are you just passing through Liberty, or do we have some time to get to—"

"Hello."

Jacob turned at the sound of Clair's voice. She'd just walked around the corner from the ladies' room. Even though the weather was humid and they'd been driving most of the day, she still looked crisp and cool in her pink tank top and denim skirt. Her timing had been so perfect just now, he wanted to kiss her.

Hell, he just wanted to kiss her.

That's all he'd seemed to be able to think about the entire day. Kissing Her. Touching her. Wondering if she was wearing the white lace bra and panties she'd bought at the department store.

Or the leopard thong. He thought a lot about that leopard thong.

He swore he was losing his mind.

"Clair, hi," he said, but hesitated when the two women looked at each other. "Ah, Clair this is Tina Holland. Tina, Clair Beauchamp. Tina works here."

Oh, for God's sake.

He'd not only just made a formal introduction between the gas station clerk and Clair, he'd made a ridiculously obvious statement.

He was definitely losing his mind.

"I'm going to be working on my car all afternoon," he said more roughly than he intended. "You'll have to find something to do on your own."

Clair watched Jacob snatch up the overalls and leave the office. She stared after him, wondering why he'd suddenly been so gruff, then realized she'd interrupted his conversation with Tina. Had he been trying to hit on the woman? Clair wondered. He'd been staring at the clerk when she'd walked around the corner, and with the ample amount of bossom the pretty redhead displayed, why wouldn't he? He'd also seemed flustered, she thought, and definitely in a hurry to leave.

Clair looked back at the clerk. Was this the kind of woman that attracted Jacob? When he'd first met Mindy, Clair was certain she'd seen interest in his eyes, too.

It was all she could do not to stare down at her own plain clothes and her uninteresting B cup. Even the new makeup she'd bought had been conservative compared to Mindy and Tina.

Maybe you need to rewrap the package, Mindy had said. Clair glanced over her shoulder, watched as Jacob tugged on the overalls, then jumped in his car, closed the hood and drove it into the gas station garage.

"Can I help you with anything?" Tina asked.

Clair blinked, then turned back to the clerk. "Yes," she said and smiled slowly. "I believe you can…"

Six

She was late.

For the tenth time in twenty minutes, Jacob stared at his watch and frowned. It was nearly seven o'clock. Clair had left a message on his motel room phone for him to meet her at Pink's Steak House at six-thirty.

So where the hell was she?

Not that he was worried. Liberty seemed to be a quiet, friendly town, and Jacob had spotted several Liberty County sheriff cars driving around this afternoon. Since Clair had told him she was going shopping on the main thoroughfare through town, and the motel they were staying at was on the same street, as well, there was no reason to be concerned.

She *did* have a knack for getting herself into situations, though, Jacob thought. All alone for the afternoon, in a strange town, a woman as naive as Clair could probably find trouble. He thought about her going into that bar last night by herself and running into Mad Dog. Though the construction worker had turned out to be a nice guy, he could have just as easily been not so nice.

Jacob's frown darkened. He stared at his watch again and signaled the cocktail waitress to bring him another beer.

He *wasn't* worried, dammit.

Tapping his fingers on the tabletop, he glanced around the dimly lit restaurant. A single pink rose in a cut glass vase and a flickering votive graced every linen covered table. Nice place, he thought, yet he still felt comfortable in his jeans and the black button-down shirt he'd pulled on after he'd scrubbed the grease from his hands and showered.

It had felt good to get his hands dirty again. He'd been so busy these past few months he'd had no time to even pick up a wrench, let alone tinker with his engine. Usually he found working on his car calmed him down, eased the stress of a difficult, and sometimes dangerous, job.

But today he'd been too distracted to relax, had found his mind drifting and his concentration shot to hell. He'd scraped his knuckles on an alternator mount and burned the inside of his forearm on the radiator. All because of Clair.

Even while he'd been covered with grease, dripping with sweat, bending over a one-hundred-twenty-degree engine, he'd had thoughts about Clair. Lurid, scandalous, erotic thoughts.

How the hell was he was going to last another three or four days? The woman was driving him crazy. Killing him.

The cocktail waitress, a shapely blonde, set another

beer in front of him, gave him a lingering smile, then left. He watched her walk away, then mentally shook his head and groaned. Last night Mindy, this morning Tina, now this waitress. Pretty women all around him, women who were clearly experienced with the opposite sex. Women he normally would have at least flirted with, maybe even more if the situation were right.

He lifted his beer and took a sip. Clair had never been the type of woman he'd been attracted to before. Naive, innocent, conservative—

Sexy?

The sip of beer in his mouth nearly went flying out as he caught sight of her moving toward him. He gulped to swallow it, then choked.

Good God, what had she done to herself?

The tight, black skirt skimming her slender hips had to be illegal in some states. Though it was well past her knees, the slit up the side seemed to expose leg all the way from the tips of her shiny black high heels clear up to her neck. Her lips were full and glossy wet, the same deep burgundy color as the sheer, long-sleeved blouse she wore. Her hair, normally straight, fell in loose, soft curls around her face and shoulders. Her eyes smoldered; her skin glowed. She kept that smoky gaze on him as she approached, exposing bare thigh with every stride.

A waiter carrying a tray of drinks caught sight of her and bumped into a chair, nearly spilling his load. His jaw slack, Jacob noticed that the rest of the men in the restaurant were staring, as well.

What the hell was she trying to do? Start a riot?

His hand tightened on his glass when she slid smoothly into the booth across from him.

"Hi," she said as if she were out of breath.

Hi? He narrowed a gaze at her. She'd walked in here looking like some kind of a sultry sex goddess and all she could say was "hi?"

He caught her scent and drew it slowly into his lungs. Dammit, she *smelled* sexy, too. Exotic and seductive.

"Sorry I'm late. I got caught up shopping this afternoon, then dropped into the hair salon and told them I wanted a new look." She pulled at one loose curl brushing her neck. "What do you think?"

What did he *think?* That it would be so easy to slide his hand up that slit in her skirt, even easier to slip off her underwear and be inside her in a matter of—

"Good evening." A pencil-necked waiter with short blond hair appeared from nowhere and gaped at Clair. "My name is George and I'll be your server this evening. May I get you something to drink?"

"Hello, George." Clair pursed her lips while she thought. "Maybe a glass of wine."

"We have a house chardonnay that's very nice." George pulled a wine list from his pocket. "And a 1995 pinot from Chile that I'm sure you'll find quite crisp and light."

Gimme a break. Jacob resisted the temptation to roll his eyes.

"Something more robust, I think," Clair breathed. "And full-bodied."

When the waiter's gaze dropped to Clair's breasts, Jacob felt a tick jump at the corner of his eye.

George blinked, then visibly swallowed. "Ah, perhaps a merlot or a cabernet?"

Clair smiled. "You pick."

"Thank you." The waiter blushed, then cleared his throat. "Yes, I will. Pick something nice, I mean."

Jacob decided that if the man didn't stop gawking at Clair, the only thing he'd pick would be his teeth from the back of his throat. When the waiter hurried away, Jacob narrowed a gaze at Clair. "I thought you were shopping for antiques today."

"I changed my mind." She shrugged a shoulder, drawing attention to the outline of a black bra under her sheer blouse. "One of those spur-of-the-moment, impulse things."

He kept his eyes on her face so he wouldn't stare at the soft swell of her breasts peeking out from the vee of her blouse. "Part of your No-Plan, Plan?"

"Absolutely." George brought her wine, but left quickly when Jacob shot him a warning look. Clair picked up her glass and sipped. "You must be hungry. What looks good on the menu?"

What looked good to him wasn't on the menu, he thought. And he was hungry, all right, but the hunger wasn't in his stomach. He would have gobbled her whole if he could have. Just watching her wet lips touch her glass made his groin ache. Made him think of other places he wanted that luscious mouth, and where he wanted his mouth on her, which was everywhere.

He'd always taken pride in his control, in his ability to take charge of a situation. It irritated the hell out of him that Clair Beauchamp could have him rolling over like a puppy wanting his tummy scratched. He'd never met a woman who could make him beg yet, and he wasn't about to start with Clair. He'd made a vow to keep his hands off her, and dammit, that's what he intended to do.

Determined that every man in this place knew she was off-limits, as well, he scanned the restaurant, saw several heads turn away when he curled his lip and all but growled. Satisfied, he buried his nose in his menu as if it were a shield of armor.

Clair glanced cautiously up at Jacob, considered telling him that his menu was upside down, but the hard set of his mouth and the twitch in the corner of his left eye warned her off. Heavens, but he was in a mood.

Not exactly the reaction she'd been hoping for.

The waiter returned and they ordered their food, then Jacob excused himself and headed toward the rest rooms.

Thank heavens.

Clair sank back in the booth on a heavy sigh of relief, then took a long sip of her wine. Her insides were still shaking from what she'd hoped would be her grand entrance. The new hairstyle and makeup had been difficult enough, but wearing a sheer blouse and skirt with a high slit had nearly caused her to hyperventilate. If ever she'd been grateful for the years of poise and self-assured composure continually pounded into her, it was now. She'd been amazed herself that she'd been able to hold her head high and that her knees hadn't crumpled under her.

What had seemed like a courageous, daring plan to gain Jacob's attention now felt silly and foolish.

Tina, from the gas station, had recommended The Head to Toe Salon and when Clair had told Bridgette, the hairdresser, that she wanted a look sexy enough to attract a man, the woman had taken on the project with the tenacity of a bulldog. The salon Clair had always gone to in Charleston, Jean-Lucs, was subdued, conservative. They served Perrier and iced mint tea while they permed and cut, played Beethoven and Bach while they colored and weaved. The Head to Toe played a country-western radio station which could barely be heard over the phones ringing, blow-dryers buzzing and the hairstylists talking over one another. It was gossip central, and in the few short hours she'd sat in the chair, Clair had learned about two affairs, three divorces and four pregnancies—one with a heated debate over who the father really was.

The afternoon had flown by. Clair's hair had been trimmed and curled, her fingernails and toes polished in WildBerry Wine. Smoke Me Blue eye shadow and RazzleDazzle lip gloss completed her makeup, then Suzie, the owner of the clothes boutique next door, brought over outfits and everyone in the place gave their opinions on what was right for Clair to catch a man. There'd been much discussion between the ladies, but they'd all finally agreed that the sheer blouse, the black, slit-up-the-side skirt, and high heels were guaranteed to bring the toughest, most hard-headed man to his knees.

So much for guarantees.

But there had been a few moments, she thought as she took another sip of her wine. When she'd walked into the restaurant, her heart pounding and her palms sweating, she'd have sworn she'd seen Jacob's mouth drop open. There'd been more than interest in his dark gaze, there'd been lust. She'd felt her hopes soar and her pulse race.

Then she'd slid into the booth and he'd been nothing but abrupt and cross.

Maybe she wasn't giving this enough of a chance, she thought. Maybe his mind was still on his car, or maybe he was hungry. She'd waited twenty-five years to seduce a man, surely she could give him a few more minutes before she...what was the term he'd used before? Oh, yes. Before she jumped his bones.

Clearly she'd gone about this all wrong. She'd been too subtle. Women who were confident, who knew what they wanted and went after it, were direct. She loosened one more button, then adjusted her blouse to expose the slightest edge of black lace. If he needed direct, then fine, she'd give him direct.

He walked back to the table at the same time their food arrived. She saw his stride falter as he looked at her, then he sat back down into the booth and dug into his food.

She took a bite of her chicken. "This is so tender," she said on a soft moan. "Would you like a taste?"

The piece of steak he'd had halfway to his mouth froze, then he glanced up at her and scowled. "No, thanks."

"Are you sure?" She took another bite, gave another sigh of pleasure. "You won't know what you're missing if you don't try it."

"Fine," he said tightly. "I'll try it."

Smiling, she speared a bite and held it out to him. Her heart all but stopped when he closed his mouth over her fork.

As strange as it seemed, that was the most erotic thing she'd ever done. Her pulse began to skip and her throat turned dry as dust.

And she could swear she'd gotten a reaction from Jacob, the kind she'd wanted. His eyes narrowed and darkened and his nostrils seemed to flare.

"So what do you think?" she asked, amazed she had any voice at all.

He stared at her for a long moment, then shrugged. "It was fine."

"That's it?" Determined to shake him up, she leaned closer, arched one eyebrow and curved her lips. "Just fine?"

His gaze dropped to the black lace she'd exposed, and he visibly swallowed. "Maybe a little better than fine."

Dammit, but the man was hardheaded. What did she have to do to break through his wall of indifference? Take her blouse off and jump on the table?

Like hell she would.

All her life she'd molded herself to suit other people, to be the person she thought someone else wanted her to be. Her mother, her father, Oliver.

And now Jacob.

She might be a fool, but she wasn't stupid.

"Thank you for meeting me for dinner, Jacob." She forced a smile. "But if you'll excuse me, I'm a little tired. I think I'll go back to the motel."

He started to push his plate away, but she shook her head. "You go on and finish your dinner. I'll see you in the morning."

"I'll just get the—"

"Don't worry about me." She slid out of the booth. "I can get myself back. You just take your time."

She quickly walked away, head held high. This time, her knees didn't tremble and her palms didn't sweat. In spite of her disappointment, she felt lighter, more comfortable in her own skin than she'd felt in her entire life.

She was almost at the front door when she heard a woman call her name. Clair saw Bridgette waving frantically from a darkened corner of the lounge area. She was with a small group of men and women.

Why not? Clair thought. She could go back to the motel, get into her pj's and watch TV, or she could spend the evening with Bridgette and her friends. She thought about the empty motel room, her empty bed, and it wasn't a difficult choice.

Smiling, she turned and walked into the lounge.

Where the hell was she?

Jacob paced irritably from Clair's motel room into his own, then back again. After he'd wolfed down the rest of his meal and paid the bill, he'd been no more than ten minutes behind her. The motel they were staying at was across the street and three doors down from the restaurant, so she couldn't have made a wrong turn.

He stared at his wristwatch, then clenched his jaw. She'd said she was tired, that she was going back to the motel. She should have been here long before him.

Dammit.

What if someone had followed her out of the restaurant? Or approached her on the street? The way she looked, she would have easily stopped traffic, not to mention caused an accident or two.

Didn't she realize the trouble she could get into dressed like that? He stomped to the motel window and looked out at the well-lit parking lot.

Nothing.

His gut twisted into a knot.

Hell, it wasn't that he hadn't liked the way she'd looked. He'd have to be dead not to appreciate the sensuality she'd radiated. What man wouldn't, for crying out loud?

But what possible reason could she have to completely change her look from cool and calm into hot and wild? And why here, in Liberty? Who would she want to impress with a new style in this small town?

He was on his way to the phone to call the front desk when it hit him like a sucker punch to the gut.

Good God, but he was an idiot.

He would have kicked himself all the way back across the street to the restaurant, but it would have taken longer for him to get there if he did. He had a pretty good idea where he'd find her.

The question was, did she *want* to be found?

"...and the kid says, 'No problem. Hillary took my backpack.'"

The crowd busted out in laughter at Bridgette's joke and Clair joined in. They'd been on a jokefest for the past ten minutes and what had started out as a small group had doubled in size, with each new member contributing a joke, a few of them risqué enough to make Clair's cheeks warm.

After Jacob's indifference to her, it felt good to be welcomed into Bridgette's group of friends. She knew a couple of the men were working their way into position to make a move on her, and while it raised her self-confidence, it didn't raise her interest.

There was only one man on her mind; only one man she wanted to be with.

Old habits died hard, she realized. She'd changed her clothing, her hair, her makeup, even the way she walked, just so Jacob would see her as a desirable woman. A woman he would want to make love to.

But as embarrassing as it was to realize she'd made a complete fool of herself, the lesson she'd learned was invaluable. From now on, she would let her heart and her gut tell her who the real Clair Beauchamp was. She would not change to please someone else, most especially a pigheaded, dim-witted private investigator from New Jersey.

While Bridgette's fiancé Pete began telling a joke about two men who had slept in a country barn for the night, Clair sipped on the drink Bridgette had insisted on buying her, something called Ride 'Em Cowboy. She'd never heard of the concoction of coffee liqueurs and vodka; she rarely drank alcohol and her parents and Oliver only drank wine or martinis.

Maybe she should let herself get a little tipsy, she thought. If only for tonight, it might get her mind off Jacob. She watched a band setting up on the other side of the lounge. Why shouldn't she dance and have some fun?

No. With a sigh, she set the drink down. She'd only regret it later if she had too much to drink, then made an idiot out of herself. She refused to have any regrets. Tonight, tomorrow or the day after. Whatever she did, she'd go into with her eyes wide open. Whatever mistakes she made, that was fine. They'd be *her* mistakes.

"…so the guy says," Pete continued, "'I don't mind at all. She died and left me a million dollars.'"

Between a mixture of groans and laughs, the cocktail waitress took new drink orders while the band announced over the microphone they'd be playing in a few moments. Steve, Pete's brother, offered to buy another drink for Clair, but she politely declined the good-looking Liberty fireman's offer. There was no point in encouraging him, not when she knew she was leaving this bar alone.

Going back to her room alone.

Still, in spite of that fact, she was ready to go back to the motel. The room would be quiet and lonely, but she'd at least have the comfort of knowing Jacob was next door.

How pathetic was she? she thought, reaching for her purse. Her only consolation, and it wasn't much, was that she knew she wasn't the first woman, and most certainly wouldn't be the last, to make a fool of herself over a man.

"Lord, have mercy." Her eyes wide, Julie, Bridgette's sister, looked over Clair's shoulder. "I think I'm in love."

"Stand in line, girlfriend," Julie's friend, Christie, gasped and stared, as well.

Clair turned and saw Jacob standing at the entrance to the lounge. His dark, narrowed gaze slowly scanned the room.

Her heart skipped a beat. Was he looking for *her?* Or was he just here, *looking* for a woman in general?

Either way, she didn't want to know. She certainly didn't need anymore rejection from Jacob, and the last thing she wanted was to see him pick up another woman.

She turned her back to him and scooted down in her seat, hoping he wouldn't spot her in the dimly lit corner. "He's coming this way." Julie sucked in a breath and leaned close to Julie and Clair. "Remember, I saw him first."

Dammit. Clair clutched her purse and clenched her teeth. If he thought he could lecture her in front of

Bridgette and her friends, he had another think coming. She refused to let him bully her or—

"Clair!" He moved beside her, put his hands on her shoulders and pulled her out of her chair. "Thank God I found you!"

While everyone looked on, Jacob dragged her close and smothered her in a hug.

"Sweetheart, I've been so worried." He laid his big hand on the back of her head and pushed her face flat against his chest. "Little Jake has been asking where his mommy is and the baby won't stop crying."

Little Jake? The baby? What in the world was he talking about?

She tried to pull away, but with her arms captured at her sides, she couldn't move. Couldn't breathe, for that matter.

"Who the hell are you?" Steve asked, starting to stand.

"Her husband." Jacob squeezed her tighter when she squeaked at his answer. Steve quickly sat back down.

"She never mentioned a husband." Bridgette eyed Jacob suspiciously. "Just that she was driving to Texas with some guy."

"We're on our way to see a specialist there for Clair's myopsia infarction," Jacob said over the music from a three-man band that had just started to play a jazzy instrumental. "When she takes her medication she can control it, but when she misses—" he shook his head sadly "—well, she forgets things."

What! Clair pushed harder to break away from Jacob's grip, but she might as well have been pushing against a brick wall.

"She forgets she has a husband and children?" Julie asked with disbelief.

Clair managed to yank her head back an inch. "Jacob, for God's sake, will you—"

He smashed her against his chest again. "Our car broke down and I had to go to the garage. I took the kids with me, and when we didn't come right back, she obviously got confused. Clair, sweetheart—" he thrust her out at arm's length "—I've been sick with worry."

She sucked in a lungful of air, ready to lambaste him, when he pulled her close again and dropped his mouth over hers. Shocked, all she could do was hold on.

It didn't seem to matter that he was simply trying to shut her up. Or even that there were several pairs of eyes watching them. All that mattered was the hot press of his lips on hers, the moist brush of his tongue.

Her pulse raced, excitement shimmered over her skin. Her fingers curled into his arms....

Dammit!

Smoothly she twisted her foot and stepped on his insole with her high heel. She felt, more than heard, the growl in his throat. He yanked away from her, his brow furrowed in pain.

"Jacob. Oh, sweetheart, I remember now." She touched his cheek tenderly. "I got sick right after you lost your job at the fertilizer plant."

"Right," he said through gritted teeth. "Now we really should get back to the kids, in case they wake up."

"And then the explosion at the fireworks plant." Clair glanced at everyone as she leaned in and whispered, "Would you ever guess he has a glass eye?"

"Never," Julie breathed, staring openmouthed at Jacob. "Which one?"

"The right one," Christie said, narrowing her gaze at Jacob.

Jacob's hand tightened on her arm. "We *really* should go now, *sweetheart.*"

"Of course." Clair picked up her purse and did her best not to smile at the sympathetic expressions on everyone's faces as they all said goodbye.

His face set tight, Jacob dragged her through the crowd, then out the front door. The night air was cool, heavy with the scent of steaks grilling from the restaurant inside, and the muted sound of Santana's "Smooth" drifted from the lounge.

She tried to break loose from his grip, but he held on tight.

"Let go of me!" she yelled at him when they hit the sidewalk.

"No." Pulling her along, he started across the street.

"How dare you say no!" With no other option, Clair stumbled behind him. "Are you crazy?"

"Obviously." When she managed to yank free, he twisted around and grabbed her by the waist, picked her up and tossed her over his shoulder.

"Jacob Carver, put me down this instant!"

"No, again," he said calmly and walked to the motel.

"You're fired," she shouted. "Terminated. Discharged. Canned. I don't ever want to—"

When he dropped her hard on her feet at his motel door, her teeth rattled.

"—see you again," she finished as he shoved his

key in the door. "You're insane. Deeply disturbed. A lunatic. Unbal—"

"Will you just shut up?" he said, then pulled her into his arms and covered her mouth with his.

Seven

If she'd had time to think, Clair might have been able to defend herself against the thrilling jolt of pleasure that slammed against her senses when Jacob's lips swept down on her own. But she couldn't think, couldn't breathe; she could only *feel*. Her arms curled around his neck, her hands moved upward and plowed into his hair. He yanked her closer, deepening the kiss as he forced her back against the door. Her entire body came alive, every nerve ending tingling with the impact of his mouth on hers. Heat coursed through her rushing blood.

She strained against him, would have climbed inside him if it were possible.

He dragged his lips from hers and blazed a trail down her neck. With a moan, her head fell to the side, offering more.

"What were you saying?" he murmured, biting the base of her earlobe.

"You're...deeply...disturbed," she said between ragged breaths.

"Very deeply." He nibbled on her throat.

"Insane." She dug her fingers into his scalp.

"Certifiable." He slid his hands around her waist, then jerked her closer.

Clair's eyes opened wide at the intimate press of his arousal against the v of her thighs. "Unbalanced," she gasped.

"Completely." He reached behind her, twisted the doorknob and they stumbled into the room.

The nightstand lamp cast shadows across the soft beige carpet and the blue floral bedspread. The tangy scent of lemon wax filled the room, and from the corner, an air conditioner hummed, lifting the ends of the sheer white drapes covering the window.

He kicked the door shut behind him and dragged her close again.

His kiss was hot and hungry, urgent. Need shivered through her. She held onto his shoulders and rose on her tiptoes, wanting more.

He'd kissed her before, but this was different. This was no-holds-barred. This was out of control.

This was pure, unbridled *passion*.

Her heart sang with the joy she felt. When he pulled his mouth from hers and moved away, left her standing alone, her eyes shot open and she felt a moment of fear that he'd changed his mind. She swayed on weak knees, watched him take two long, quick strides to the drapes and snap them closed.

Then he was back again, his arms around her, his heat seeping into her, his tongue sliding over her parted lips, then rushing inside. She met him eagerly, opened to him, felt her blood pounding through her veins.

As one, they moved toward the bed.

This time when he kissed her, he slowed the pace a bit, lingered on the corner of her mouth, a leisurely exploration. While one hand fisted into her hair at the back of her head, the other slid down her arm, then slipped inside the high slit of her skirt.

She trembled.

"I've wanted to do that from the first moment I saw you walk in the restaurant," he said hoarsely, skimming the outer skin of her thigh with his fingertips.

Why didn't you? she wanted to ask, but she couldn't think, couldn't speak. Intense arrows of pleasure shot through her. She felt dizzy and hot. And then he cupped her buttocks, pulled her closer to the hard bulge at the front of his jeans, and every thought flew out of her head.

She rose up on her toes, pressing against him, then lowered herself slowly down.

He moaned.

"Clair," His voice was ragged and hoarse. "Are you sure about this?"

"Yes," she whispered, wondered how he could even ask.

"Look at me." He cupped her face in his hands. "No doubts?"

She shook her head, laid her hands on his broad chest, felt the rapid beating of his heart. "No doubts."

"Good."

Her knees hit the edge of the bed and they tumbled

backward, sank into the mattress. While his mouth tasted the base of her throat, he dipped under her skirt again and slid his callused palm down her thigh. Whimpering, she lifted her hips upward. He tugged her zipper open, then slid the garment away.

She reached to slip her heels off, but he took her hand and held it down on the bed. "Leave them on a minute. I want to look at you."

Clair felt her cheeks flush, but the look in Jacob's eyes as his gaze slid from her black lace underwear, slowly down her bare legs, all the way to the tips of her black high heels, excited her beyond anything she could have ever imagined.

When his hand followed the same path as his gaze, her heart skipped, then raced.

Closing her eyes, she laid her head back and let herself savor the rough slide of his fingers over her skin. Fire raced up and down her entire body. One by one, her heels dropped to the floor. Then his hand moved back up, over her calf…her thigh. He hesitated at the lacy edge of her underwear, brushed the tips of his fingers back and forth, moved upward again. Breath held, heart pounding, she felt him unbutton her blouse. When the sheer fabric parted, he flattened his hand over her bare belly. She quivered at his gentle touch.

"You're so smooth." His voice was rough. "So soft."

Sensation after sensation swirled through her. Ribbons of bright colors, a tapestry of textures. The scent of man and woman and passion.

And then his hands closed over her breasts.

On its own, her body bowed slightly upward as she pressed herself more fully into him. Her breath came in short, ragged gasps as he kneaded her soft flesh. A fever built between her legs, a pulsing, throbbing pressure that demanded release. She wanted more, was certain she'd die if he didn't hurry.

When she reached for the buttons on his shirt, he smiled and shook his head. "Not yet."

Jacob knew he'd lose it completely if he didn't keep some kind of barrier between them. He wanted to take his time, to make this last, though he wasn't so certain he could. Not with those soft little sounds of needs she was making, and the way her long, tempting body kept squirming under him.

When her fingers slid down his chest and moved toward the snap of his jeans, he snagged her wrist and lifted it over her head, then captured her other wrist and pulled it over her head, as well. If she touched him, it would be all over.

He wanted more.

With his free hand, he flicked open the front clasp of her black lace bra and bared her breasts.

Then he did nearly lose it.

She was perfect. Her breasts were full and firm, her skin flushed, soft as rose petals. Her chest rose and fell rapidly. Fire raced through his blood, pounded in his temple.

He wanted like he'd never wanted before. He lowered his head to take.

When his mouth closed over the pebbled, rosy tip of her breast, she arched upward on a gasp. He pulled her deeper into his mouth, slid his tongue back and forth over her nipple. It grew harder.

So did he.

Ignoring the insistent ache in his groin, he kept his attention on Clair, tasted her sweetness. She moaned deeply, moved restlessly under him. When he moved to her other breast, she whimpered. He suckled her, flicked his thumb over the damp nipple he'd just abandoned, felt the bud tighten even more under the rough texture of his skin.

"Jacob, *please*." Clair choked out the words.

"Not yet," he murmured.

He released her hands, then moved down her belly. He heard her breath catch in her throat, then her fingers drove into his hair. He wasn't certain if she were trying to tug him back up or hold him still.

He didn't care.

He slid his hands under her hips, blazed kisses over her belly, explored the curves and valleys with his tongue. Then he moved lower still.

He felt her body tighten, tremble with need and uncertainty. He nipped at the edge of black lace, then slid the thin swatch of fabric down her hips, down her legs. He caressed her with his hands, nibbled on her hipbone. Then lower.

Her body felt like liquid fire. When he dipped into the sweetness of her body with the tip of his tongue, the breath she'd been holding rushed out on a deep, low moan. He stroked her, made love to her with his mouth. Mindless, she lifted her hips, rolled her head from side to side on a deep moan.

"*Jacob!*" She twisted under him on a sob. "*Now.* Please now."

"Yes." He moved quickly, knowing he couldn't last. He practically tore his shirt away, barely got the rest of his clothes off. He kneed her legs apart, took her hips in his hands, then entered her fast and hard.

He heard her cry out, hesitated, but when she wrapped her legs and arms around him and moved against him, he couldn't think at all. He moved inside the tight, hot, velvet glove of her body. Never had he felt anything so intense, so exquisite. So perfect.

She met him thrust for thrust, dug her fingernails into his back. They strained together, desperately, wildly.

He felt her climax shatter through her in violent waves of heat and pleasure. Her arms came tightly around his neck, held on.

He let himself go, groaned as his own body found release. He thrust deeply, shuddering, then fell over the edge with her.

Amazing.

Sprawled across the bed, across each other, Clair waited for her heart to slow and her breath to even out.

She couldn't move.

Unbelievably amazing.

Jacob had rolled to his side, but he still had one arm and one leg draped over her. His skin was damp, his breathing as erratic as her own.

"Damn," he muttered.

She smiled, deciding that the single swear word was a compliment.

"I didn't get that blouse off you," he said, his voice thick and hoarse. "I really wanted to get that blouse off you."

He shifted, pulled her snugly against him, stroked her hair away from her face, then pressed his lips lightly to her temple. A moment passed, long and silent, then Jacob finally spoke. "You could have told me, Clair."

She laid her hand on his chest, felt the heavy thud of his heart against her palm. "That I was a virgin?"

"No. That you have a freckle in the shape of a poodle in the middle of your back."

She yanked away from him. "I most certainly do—"

"For God's sake, I'm kidding." He pulled her back into his arms. "Yes. That you were a virgin."

"I was afraid you wouldn't—that you might not—" Her gaze dropped. "That you wouldn't want me."

His chuckle rumbled deep in his chest. "Sweetheart, of all the things to be afraid of, trust me, that's not one you need to concern yourself with."

"Then it wouldn't have mattered to you?" she asked. "Given you one more reason to stay away from me?"

"Maybe." He kissed each cheek, then the tip of her nose. "But sooner or later, this would have happened even if I had known. One more day in the car with you and I think I would have pulled off the road, dragged you in the back seat and taken you right there."

Just the thought of him doing that made her pulse pick up again. "Really?"

"Really. When you walked into the restaurant tonight, I nearly swallowed my tongue."

Though her cheeks warmed, pleasure swelled in her chest. She slid her hand to his arm and brushed her fingers back and forth over his muscular biceps. "I was hoping I'd get your attention."

He sighed, then rolled to his back, pulling her on top of him. "You didn't need to change a thing about yourself to get my attention. You've had my complete attention from the second you stepped out of that bridal shop.''

"The bridal shop?'' Her eyes widened in surprise. "But I was engaged, practically married. You didn't know me at all.''

"Practically married is not married,'' he said, shaking his head in disbelief. "And you're not *that* naive, Clair, to think a man has to know a woman to fantasize about taking her to bed.''

He'd fantasized about her? The idea made her stomach flutter. Folding her arms over his chest, she gazed down at him. "No, I suppose not. I just haven't been around a lot of men, and Oliver was, well, I suppose he was a bit conservative. He thought we should wait until after we were married to sleep together.''

Frowning, he slid his hands up her shoulders, then down her back. "Oliver is an idiot.''

Surprised by Jacob's bitter tone, Clair lifted a brow. "You don't even know him. Why would you say that?''

His dark gaze met and held hers for a long moment. She had the oddest feeling he was about to tell her something, then suddenly he flipped her onto her back.

"Let's just say I know his type,'' he said tightly. "And anyway, he'd have to be an idiot to let you go.''

It was the nicest thing Jacob had ever said to her, Clair realized. She had to swallow the thickness in her throat before she could speak. "He didn't let me go,'' she said quietly. "I ran away and left him standing in the church. It must have been awful for him.''

Jacob's mouth pressed into a hard line and his eyes searched hers. "Are you having regrets?"

"Guilt, maybe." She reached up and touched his lips with her fingertips. "But no regrets. There isn't one thing I would change that's happened to me since I left that church."

"Not one thing?" He took her hand in his, kissed each fingertip. Every soft press of his lips sent sparks of electricity buzzing up her arm. "You sure?"

It rushed through her like a warm wind, the need, the heat, the desire. Her heart began to pound; her breath caught. "Well…maybe one thing…"

He hesitated, lifted a brow as he glanced down at her.

"I would have preferred four children instead of two," she said thoughtfully. "Little Jake and the baby—oh, dear, I can't remember, is it a boy or a girl?"

It was easier, Clair thought, to let herself tease, to be playful rather than discuss Oliver. Her ex-fiancé was the *last* person she wanted to think about right now. And certainly the last person she wanted to talk about.

One corner of Jacob's mouth curved. He turned his attention to the inside of her elbow. "A boy. Trevor."

"Of course, Trevor." She sucked in a breath when his teeth nipped at the sensitive skin. "Well, Jake and Trevor are getting older and with my disease—what was it again?"

His hand moved up her belly, his knuckles brushed the soft underside of her breast. "Myopia infarction."

"That's it." She gripped the bedclothes in her fists and hung on. "Well, I keep forgetting where I've put the children, so it would help if we had a couple more so they could all keep an eye on each other." She arched upward when his thumb brushed back and forth over her nipple. "And you…know…how much I want a little girl."

"Soon as I get my job back at the fertilizer plant," he said hoarsely, "we'll talk about it."

He moved over her, his hands, his mouth, brought her to the brink slowly this time. Mindlessly, breathlessly, they held on to each other, then once again slipped over the edge.

She was already in the shower when he woke the next morning. *His* shower, he noted, opening first one heavy eyelid, then the other. He blinked hard, then glanced at the nightstand clock.

7:00 a.m.?

With a groan, he slammed his eyes shut again. The woman got up too damn early.

He rolled away from the bathroom door and pulled the covers over his head, but he could still hear the spray of the water and the sound of Clair singing. Something familiar, though he couldn't place it or make out the words. He dragged the blanket down and listened, then opened his eyes again and flopped onto his back. She was singing in French. Something from an opera, he guessed, though he wouldn't know one from the other.

Thank God.

He could picture Clair, her back perfectly straight as she sat in one of those private theater boxes. She'd be dressed in sleek black, her shiny, dark hair pulled up in a knot on top of her head, exposing that long, regal neck of hers.

That was her world. The only world she knew.

She'd have her adventure, mix with the common folk for a few days, then she'd go back to that world. Where she belonged.

And he didn't.

Furrowing his brow, he sat and scrubbed a hand over his face. Where in the hell had *that* thought come from?

He and Clair both knew that they would go their own ways once they got to Wolf River. Last night hadn't changed that.

He glanced at the bathroom door and frowned. It *hadn't* changed, he told himself. The only thing it changed was that they'd be sleeping in one bed until they got to Wolf River. Now that he'd had a taste of her, there was no way he could keep his hands off her.

He couldn't remember when he'd ever been so hungry for a woman before.

So *desperate*.

When he heard her voice crack on a high note, Jacob shook his head, then tossed the covers off. Naked, he headed for the bathroom.

She'd switched from opera to country-western, he noted, a Dixie Chicks tune about wide-open spaces, though she wasn't quite getting the words right.

Her song was cut off abruptly by an explosion of cursing.

Lifting a brow, he inched the door open. "Clair?"

When she didn't answer, he stepped inside. On the other side of the blue plastic shower curtain, all he could see was her head stuck under the shower, her face lifted to the spray. He moved beside her.

"Something wrong?"

She squeaked, grabbing the shower curtain and hiding behind it. "Jacob! You scared me!"

"I thought you were hurt." He tried to peek around the curtain, but couldn't see a thing. "First all that caterwauling, then you're cursing like a truck driver with a loose wheel."

"Caterwauling!" She stuck her head out. Her face was wet, her cheeks flushed. Her eyes dropped to his naked body, widened, then she snapped her gaze back up. "First of all, I got shampoo in my eyes, and second, I'll have you know I studied with Mademoiselle Marie Purdoit for three years. She said I was a natural."

"Maybe she meant your hair," he teased.

Frowning, Clair swiped a hand over her face, flicked the water at him, then ducked behind the curtain and started to sing "Love Me Tender" in a deep, exaggerated off-key voice.

So she wanted to play, did she?

Grinning, he ducked back into his room and grabbed his camera, then slipped back into the bathroom and took aim.

"Clair," he said loudly. "I'm sorry if I hurt your feelings. You sing very well for someone who's tone-deaf."

"Tone-deaf!"

As she stuck her head out again, he clicked the picture. Shocked, she stood there for a moment, her mouth and eyes open wide. He took another shot.

With a shriek, she disappeared behind the curtain.

And cursed profusely.

Laughing, he put the camera aside. "Make way, Mademoiselle Beauchamp. I'm coming in."

"Jacob Carver," she yelled as he stepped inside the shower, "if you dare to—"

He cut her words off by taking hold of her shoulders and dropping his mouth on hers. She drew in a startled breath, then her arms came around his shoulders.

In spite of the busy night they'd had, the need rose instantly, heated his blood and made his heart race. He turned his back to the hot spray as he deepened the kiss and pulled her against him. Her skin was hot and smooth and wet. Her breasts flattened against his chest as she rose up to meet him; her arms tightened around his neck while she curled one long, smooth leg behind his.

Gasping, she dragged her mouth from his and looked up at him, her eyes filled with desire. "Tell me what to do."

He slid his hands down to her bottom and lifted her. "Wrap your legs around my waist."

He entered her quickly, pressed her back against the cool tile, was deep inside her when he began to move. Her moan echoed off the shower walls.

When her head fell back, he dragged his mouth and teeth along her jaw. Her long, sleek, wet legs tightened around him, intensifying the pleasure until it became unbearable.

"Jacob...hurry..."

Liquid fire raced through over his skin, pulsed through his veins. He felt the bite of her fingernails in his shoulders, then the nip of her teeth. He thrust deeper still, felt her tighten around him, tremble.

Her shudder rolled through him. With a moan, he followed.

Barely able to breathe, he eased her down his body,

felt her body sag against him when her feet touched the tub floor.

Steam swirled around them and the hot spray battered their bodies. Still dazed, he gathered her close for a moment, then turned off the water and took her back to his bed.

Eight

"Coffee?"

"Hmm." Afraid she might fall off the cloud she was presently floating on, Clair did not turn her head at Jacob's question or even open her eyes. Since the shower incident almost two hours ago, she and Jacob had made love, dozed off in each other's arms, then made love again.

She had a bruise on her hip, knots in her damp hair, and every muscle in her entire body ached.

Smiling, she slid deeper under the sheet covering her and burrowed into the mattress.

"I take it that's a yes." He touched his lips to her bare shoulder, nibbled for a moment, then rolled off the bed. "I think we're both going to need it black and strong today."

Slitting one eye open, Clair watched Jacob drag a pair of jeans up his long, powerful legs, then tug the denim over his tight, firm butt. His waist was narrow, his shoulders wide, his arms muscular. He seemed completely at ease with his body, naked or clothed, and completely at ease with himself.

She envied him that. She'd always felt awkward with her body. Her arms and legs had always seemed too long, her breasts too small, her shoulders too bony. Well, at least until last night she'd felt that way. Now she felt…just right.

Not perfect, as everyone had wanted her to be, but just right.

"Thank you," she said softly.

"You can thank me when I get back." He pulled on a long-sleeved navy-blue shirt and waggled his eyebrows at her while he closed the buttons.

As spent and consumed as she felt, her body still tingled at the thought. Rolling to her side, she propped her head up in the palm of her hand and smiled at him. "Not for the coffee, for last night." She felt a blush work its way up her neck. "It was wonderful. You were wonderful."

Grinning, he sat back down on the edge of the bed and brushed his lips over hers. "You were pretty damn wonderful yourself, Miss Beauchamp."

"Why, thank you, Mr. Carver." She laid her palm on his knee. "How kind of you to say so."

He leaned into the kiss, increased the pressure of his mouth on hers. "Don't mention it."

She felt his thigh muscles tighten and bunch as she moved her hand up his leg. When he pressed her back onto the mattress, she forgot every ache, forgot her exhaustion. Pleasure heated her skin, her blood, made her heart pump furiously.

Jacob moved his mouth down her throat, blazed hot kisses while his hand tugged the sheet slowly down—

The phone on the nightstand rang.

"Dammit." Jacob lifted his head and frowned at the phone. "That will be Odell. I was supposed to be at the garage thirty minutes ago to help drop the radiator back in my car."

Clair slid her hands smoothly down his chest, lingered at the open snap of his jeans. "You should probably answer it."

She watched his gaze darken and his eyes narrow when she traced her fingertip down his zipper. Her boldness shocked, yet thrilled her at the same time.

"You answer it," he said roughly, then lowered his head to her neck while his hands tugged the sheet away. "Tell him I'm on my way."

Breathless, her head spinning, she answered the phone on the fourth ring.

"Clair?"

Her heart, which had been pounding so fiercely, stopped.

"Oliver?"

Jacob went still, then lifted his head and met her startled gaze. His mouth pressed into a hard line, and he rolled away.

"Why are you answering Carver's phone?" Oliver demanded. "Put him on the line."

"How did you know where I was?" Clair pulled the sheet up to cover herself, watched Jacob yank a pair of socks out of his bag, then grab his boots and sit on the edge of the bed.

"It doesn't matter how I know," Oliver said irritably.

In spite of everything, Clair was certain her mother

hadn't given the number to Oliver. "It matters to me."

"I just happened to see the number written down in your mother's office."

"You went through my mother's office?" She sat, stared at Jacob's stiff back while he pulled his boots on and laced them.

"You've forced me to resort to underhanded measures to find you." Oliver's tone was pious. "Clair, you're jeopardizing your reputation by gallivanting around the country with this Carver fellow. He's not to be trusted."

Clair frowned at the phone. "Why would you say that?"

"Men like Jacob Carver have no sense of ethics or scruples. They'll say and do anything to get what they want. He may even attempt to seduce you by telling you lies about me."

"I assure you, that has not happened." If anything, the opposite was true—she'd seduced Jacob. But Oliver didn't need to know that.

"I insist you come back home immediately." His irritation snapped across the line. "We can be married in a quiet ceremony."

"Oliver." Clair reminded herself that after everything she'd done, the way she'd left him in the lurch, he deserved her patience. "I know my parents explained to you I'm going to meet my brothers in Wolf River. I don't know when I'm coming home."

"You're being ridiculous," he said with more than a touch of arrogance in his voice. "There's still time to repair the damage you've done to our social standing. It's understandable that you've had a temporary breakdown from the shock of learning about your adoption. Just come home, Clair, and I'll forgive you everything. I love you.''

She'd thought he had, but the words sounded empty now. It seemed to Clair that Oliver's ''social standing'' was what troubled him the most. She knew she should be hurt, but the fact was, she was relieved.

When Jacob stood and strode across the room, Clair reached a hand out to stop him, but he didn't look back. The chain beside the door rattled when he slammed it behind him.

With a sigh, she laid back on the bed and stared at the ceiling.

''Clair?'' Oliver's impatient voice came over the line again. ''Answer me. Are you there? *Clair!*''

''I appreciate your magnanimous offer,'' she said evenly. ''But my answer is no. I did not have a temporary breakdown, I am not coming home, and I am not going to marry you. Goodbye, Oliver.''

''Clair—''

She hung up the phone, then took it off the hook. When she heard the phone ringing from her room, she groaned and put a pillow over her head.

Furrowing her brow, she pulled her head back out from under the pillow and listened to the persistent ring.

Why had Oliver asked the motel desk to connect him with Jacob's room first? she wondered. He'd obviously been surprised when she'd said hello, so he hadn't expected her to answer the phone. And he'd asked her to put Jacob on the phone.

Why had he done that?

Maybe Oliver had thought he could convince Jacob to bring her back to South Carolina. Perhaps offer him a reward for her return.

It didn't matter, she thought, thankful when the phone finally stopped ringing. Whatever Oliver's reasons were for wanting to speak to Jacob, she simply didn't care.

She knew that Jacob would be headed back to New Jersey soon, if not immediately, after they arrived in Wolf River. They might have slept together, but she wasn't so foolish as to think that last night had changed anything for him.

And she certainly wasn't so foolish as to tell him that she'd fallen in love with him. No doubt she'd be left standing in a spray of gravel and a cloud of dust if she did.

With a sigh, she looked at the nightstand clock, watched the time change from 9:02 to 9:03. She had no intention of pining away the precious minutes and seconds they had left together. Whatever time they had, she was determined to make the most of it.

Sliding out of bed, she hurried into her room and dug through her suitcase. She pulled out the leopard print thong, smiled slowly, then headed for the shower.

Two hours later, covered with dirt and sweat, Jacob came back to an empty, quiet motel room. Disappointment stabbed at him that Clair wasn't exactly where he'd left her—in his bed—but he supposed it was for the best. It was nearly noon and if they were going to make any time on the road at all today, they'd need to get a move-on.

Unbuttoning his shirt, he headed toward her room and stuck his head in. "Clair?"

Her room was empty, as well. His disappointment

turned to irritation. Where the hell had she taken off to now?

Her bed was neatly made, the nightstands clear.

And her suitcase was missing.

His heart slammed against his ribs.

Oliver.

A muscle jumped in the corner of Jacob's eye. He shouldn't have left her alone, dammit. Especially after last night. Clair was vulnerable, maybe having regrets. That idiot Oliver had probably bullied her, played on her guilt and talked her into returning to Charleston.

He'd strangle the bastard.

Clair was too damn trusting. Maybe he should have told her about Oliver messing around with that blond bimbo, that the two of them had been at the Wanderlust Motel the night before the wedding and the night before that, too.

That certainly would have blown all her wide-eyed innocence to hell.

Which was exactly why he *hadn't* told her. He couldn't remember when he'd met a woman with such enthusiasm for life, such honesty. A woman who blushed so easily, laughed so heartily and trusted without question.

Fists clenched, he strode into the bathroom, looking for something, anything, she might have left behind. A brush, a tube of lipstick, a razor.

But there was nothing. Because she'd stayed in his room last night and used his shower this morning, even her motel soap was unopened, the glass still in its plastic wrapper, the shampoo still on the counter. As if she'd never been here at all.

She'd gotten to him, dammit. Gotten under his

skin. No woman had ever done that before. Not like this.

Dammit, *dammit.*

Well, fine, then. He set his teeth. He thought he'd seen beneath her submissive rich-girl facade and glimpsed a stronger, more determined, decisive woman. Obviously he'd been wrong.

Swearing under his breath, he tore at the buttons of his shirt and headed back toward his own room. If she wanted to go, then good riddance. He'd never wanted to go traipsing around these backroads, anyway. He hoped she and Oliver and his blond bimbo would be happy. *"Hasta la vista, baby,"* he said tightly. *"Sai la vie, Auf Wied—"*

"Who are you talking to?"

He turned so fast at the sound of her voice behind him, he whacked his elbow on the doorjamb. A jolt of numbing electricity shot up his arm. The single word he uttered was raw and coarse.

"Well, for heaven's sake." Key still in her hand, Clair stood in the open doorway of her motel room. "What's wrong with you?"

Momentarily dumbstruck at the sight of her, Jacob simply stared. She'd dressed to suit the hot day, a black tank top, tan capris and a pair of sandals with a white daisy between the toes.

Relief poured through him.

Followed quickly by annoyance.

"Where the hell were you?"

She lifted a brow, then closed the door behind her. "You didn't see my note?"

Note? He glanced back at his room. He'd been too busy ranting about her leaving to consider she hadn't actually left, or that she might have written a note.

"Obviously not." She dropped her black shoulder bag onto the bed, then crossed her arms as she faced him. "You thought I left, didn't you?"

"No."

"Liar."

"All right." He shifted awkwardly. "So maybe I did. Just for a minute or so."

"You really thought I would do that? Leave without saying goodbye?"

"You were talking to Oliver when I left." He defended himself. "Your suitcase is gone. What the hell was I supposed to think?"

"My suitcase—" she kept her gaze level with his as she walked toward him "—is right next to yours, in *your* room—the same room I put the note in."

When she moved past him and disappeared into his room, he shoved his hands into his pockets and followed.

Snatching a note off the bed, she stuck it in his face. "If you would have taken a moment to look instead of jumping to conclusions, you would have noticed."

Jacob, her note read, *Went to see Bridgette. Be back shortly.*

"Oh." Dammit. The only thing he hated more than being wrong about something, was having it waved under his nose. "Well, okay. I'll just take a shower and we'll hit the road."

"Not so fast, Carver."

"What?"

"I believe you owe me an apology."

There actually *was* something he hated more than having a mistake waved under his nose—saying he was sorry. "For what?"

She folded her arms and lifted her chin. "Based on erroneous information, you made an *assumption* that I'd packed my bag and left without so much as a thank you. That is a hardly a compliment to my character, and it speaks volumes of your faith in me."

"All right." He scowled at her. "I shouldn't have *assumed*."

She lifted a brow. "That's my apology?"

"Take it or leave it."

Rolling her eyes, she sighed and moved close to him. "Do you want to know what Oliver and I talked about?"

"No."

"Okay." She turned to walk away.

He grabbed her arm and dragged her back, though he was too dirty to haul her against him the way he wanted to. Damn her to hell, anyway.

"Yes," he said through clenched teeth.

"He said we could still get married in a quiet ceremony, that he would forgive me everything."

"What a generous guy." Jacob's voice was hard enough to cut granite.

"He said we could save our social situation if we told everyone I had a breakdown after I found out I was adopted."

"He's an idiot." Jacob decided he just might take a trip back to Charleston after all. He'd like to see Oliver's face just before he slammed a fist into his nose. "What else did he say?"

"That I shouldn't trust you." Clair dropped her gaze as she ran a finger down the front of Jacob's open shirt. "He said that men like you seduce women like me."

His pulse jumped when she tugged his shirt from

his jeans. "Maybe you shouldn't trust me," he said evenly. "Maybe I will seduce you."

His blood drained from his head and shot straight to his groin when she reached for the snap on his jeans.

"Too late," she all but purred as she tugged his zipper down. "I seduced you first."

"Is that what happened?"

"That's exactly what happened."

"Clair." He covered her hand with his to hold her still. "I need to take a shower."

She pressed her lips to his. "How long will that take you?"

"You know that town we were in two days ago?"

"Plug Nickel?"

"Don't Blink."

Careful not to brush up against her, he kissed her hard, nearly forgot his good intentions, then yanked his mouth from hers and headed for the shower, pulling clothes off on his way. The water was still cold as he soaped up, but it did nothing to cool the fire burning in his blood.

"Jacob?"

He smiled at her impatience, stuck his head out to tell her to join him if she couldn't wait.

The camera flashed.

He swore, reached out a hand to grab her.

She jumped back and the camera flashed again. Laughing, she hurried out of the bathroom before he came out after her.

He was going to wring her neck, he told himself.

Right after he'd made love to her.

Nine

The two-lane highway stretched long and flat under a hot sun. Fields of alfalfa on one side of the road gave the air a sweet, earthy scent. Until the breeze shifted. Then the pungent scent of cow from the dairy farm on the other side of the highway gained dominance.

Clair rested her arms on the door frame of the open car window and breathed in deeply. Cow or alfalfa, it didn't matter. With the sun on her face, the wind in her hair, and Jacob humming along with a Billy Joel song beside her, what could possibly matter? Nature was a beautiful thing. Even the dark, thick clouds gathering on the distant horizon didn't worry her.

Life was wonderful.

They'd been on the road for three hours since they'd left Liberty. To Jacob's annoyance, she'd made him stop several times so she could take pictures: a white steepled church in a tiny town called Hat Box; an abandoned tractor covered with moon-flower vine in a meadow outside of Bobcat; an old barn in Eunice. She couldn't wait to see them developed.

Especially the picture she'd taken of Jacob in the shower this morning.

The expression of shock on his face, then anger, had been priceless. Definitely a "Kodak moment." Though he'd grumbled about the surprise photo, she'd told him that turnabout was fair play. He'd taken two of her; she'd taken two of him. They were Even Steven, as the saying went.

Somehow, Jacob hadn't quite seen it that way, but after he'd stepped out of the shower, they'd both forgotten soon enough about the pictures.

Their minds—and their hands—had been occupied elsewhere.

He'd told her before that she was naive, but she wasn't so naive to think that what she and Jacob had shared wasn't something exceptional. Something special. She was certain she would never know another lover like him. That she would never love another man the same way she loved Jacob. Though her mind told her she *would* love again, her heart wasn't so certain.

The wind whipped at the ends of her hair and the late afternoon sun warmed her cheeks. In spite of the ache in her heart, she smiled.

There were no regrets. If their relationship was to be no more than a physical one, then she would live that. She would be *happy* with that. Well, if not happy, then at least content.

Tucking her chin into her hands, she closed her eyes and let her mind drift.

What if it were possible that there *could* be more for them? she wondered. That maybe, just *maybe* Jacob had feelings for her that could take them past these few short days?

He'd been angry this morning because he'd thought she'd packed up and returned to Charleston after speaking to Oliver. Was he angry because he cared about her? She'd seen something in his eyes beyond anger when she'd come back to the motel room. Relief maybe? Jealousy?

She sighed, then shook her head.

She'd only make herself crazy if she tried to second guess what Jacob's feelings for her might be. She was having enough trouble with her *own* feelings, for heaven's sake. She knew she would only be setting herself up for disappointment if she let herself hope that Jacob might want more.

"So what's it gonna be, Clair?"

Startled by Jacob's question, she jerked her head around. "What?"

"We'll need to stop in an hour or so. Maybe sooner if that storm comes in." He picked up the map lying on the seat between them and held it out to her. "Where this time?"

"Oh." Settling back in her seat, she found where they were at the moment, then studied the towns lying ahead of them.

Forest Glen? No, too generic. Rolling Flats? A contradiction of terms if ever she'd heard one. Crab Apple? Too tart.

Gray Creek…Arrow Bend…Quartz.

No. No. No.

Fifty miles west, she found it.

Smiling, she looked up at Jacob and held out the map.

An hour later, Jacob pulled into the parking lot of The Forty Winks Motel in Lucky, Louisiana. Thick, dark clouds had already soaked up the light before the sun had even gone down. The air was hot and heavy and still, charged with electricity.

When thunder rumbled in the distance, Clair shuddered, then grabbed her purse and followed Jacob into the motel office.

The clerk behind the desk, an elderly woman with gold chains on her thick glasses and tight gray curls on her head, dozed in a corner chair. Curled in the woman's wide lap was a fat tabby cat, who opened one eye when Jacob and Clair walked in, then closed it again. From a small color TV, the sound of a popular game show blasted out questions in rapid-fire succession.

"...'Then there was bad weather'...was the opening line for this Hemmingway story..."

"Moveable Feast," Jacob muttered.

Clair glanced at Jacob, who didn't appear to be aware that he'd answered the question. When the game-show host gave the answer and Jacob was correct, Clair lifted a brow.

While they waited politely for the clerk to realize she had customers, the questions from the television continued. "This is the eighth planet out from the earth," the host said.

"Neptune." Jacob tugged his wallet out of his jean's back pocket.

Clair raised both brows.

"What is the square root of twenty-five thousand?"

"Fifty."

Her mouth open, Clair stared at Jacob, who tapped his palm down on the counter bell. The clerk came awake with a small snort. The cat tumbled off the woman's lap, then looked at Jacob and twitched his tail.

"Dear me." A hand on her ample bosom, the clerk jumped up and pushed her glasses back up her long nose. She wore a silver-metal name tag that said Dorothy. "I must have nodded off."

"We'd like a room for the night." Jacob slid a credit card across the counter. "King-size bed, non-smoking."

A room, as in *one.* Clair released the breath she'd been holding. Though they'd shared a bed last night, nothing had been said between them today regarding the sleeping arrangements for tonight.

How strange it was that she'd never checked into a motel room with a man before, and yet with Jacob it felt so comfortable, so natural to her.

The cat jumped up on the counter and glared at Jacob. Jacob glared back. A big, round blue ID tag on the cat's collar said Zeke.

When Zeke turned his back on Jacob and sauntered over to Clair to have his head scratched, Jacob scowled.

"Welcome to Lucky," the woman said with a friendly smile while she ran the credit card. "Where you and your wife headed?"

Your wife. Clair glanced sideways at Jacob, waited for him to correct the woman.

He simply signed the credit-card slip Dorothy

handed to him and slid it back across the counter. "Wolf River."

"Why, fancy that." The clerk scanned two card keys, then passed them to Jacob. "I have a cousin in Wolf River."

Clair looked up sharply. "You—you have a cousin there?"

"Why, yes. Boyd Smith. His wife's name is Angela."

Clair's heart started to pound like a drum. "Have you been there?" she asked softly. "To Wolf River?"

"Used to spend every summer there on my aunt and uncle's ranch outside of town." Dorothy's smile widened. "'Course that was more than fifty years ago, but I've been back to visit Boyd and Angie a few times. Hardly recognize the town it's grown so."

"Clair." Jacob touched her shoulder. "Maybe you should wait."

She looked at him, then shook her head and glanced back at the clerk. "Do you...have you ever heard of the Blackhawk family?"

"The Blackhawks?" The woman seemed surprised by the question. "Well, of course. Anyone's ever been to Wolf River County has heard of the Blackhawks. They used to own more than half the land south of town."

"Used to?"

"There were three brothers when I was a teenager," Dorothy said. "William was the oldest. He had a mean spirit, that one. Then there was Jonathan and Thomas. Jonathan was the quiet one and Thomas was the hothead. I used to fancy Thomas when I was a teenager," Dorothy said with a bat of her eyes, then leaned across the counter and pressed her lips into a thin line. "Never believed he tried to kill that man, even though he went to prison for it and ended up dying there, poor man. Took almost twenty years to prove him innocent."

Her uncles, Clair realized. William and Thomas.

And her father was Jonathan.

"Did you—" Clair had to swallow the thickness in her throat "—did you know Jonathan?"

"Met him a couple of times one summer when I worked part-time at the hardware store. We were both teenagers back then." With a sigh, Dorothy scratched Zeke's head. "Angela sent me the newspaper article about the car accident. Killed his whole family—three little ones and his wife, though I can't remember her name."

We're not all dead, Clair thought. *We're alive.*

"Norah," Clair whispered. "Her name was Norah."

"That's right." Dorothy looked up in surprise. "You know the Blackhawks?"

"No." She shook her head. "I—I've heard of them."

"Far as I know, Thomas's son Lucas is the only one left now," Dorothy said sadly. "There was talk about William's boy, but the way I heard it, he ran off when he was a teenager and no one's seen him in years."

When the phone rang and Dorothy turned to answer it, Jacob took hold of Clair's arm. "We should go."

Outside the office, Clair sagged against Jacob. He circled his arms around her and held her close.

"I'd seen the documents," she said quietly. "Listened to my parents' admission. But, until this moment, it never seemed real to me." She curled her fingers into the front of his shirt and looked up at him. "That woman in there just made it real."

"Yeah." He tucked her hair behind her ears. "It's real."

"She met my father." The wonder of it had her smiling. And crying. "Knew my uncles."

A humid breeze blew over them; thunder rumbled, closer than it had been before. They stood there for a long, silent moment, then she touched Jacob's cheek, needed to know that he was real, too. His skin was warm, the stubble of his beard sent tingles up her arm. When he pressed his lips to her palm, butterflies danced in her stomach.

Something shifted. In the air. Between them. In the Universe, Clair thought. When Jacob's eyes narrowed and darkened, she thought he felt it, too.

But then he dropped his hands away and shoved them into his front jean's pockets. "There's a pizza place across the street," he said evenly. "Why don't we get something to eat?"

"All right." She forced her tone to be light and her smile to be bright. "As long as it's double pepperoni."

"Pepperoni was on the forbidden list?" Jacob shook his head in disgust. "That's downright cruel."

"Tell me about it."

They crossed the street to a two-story brick building—Earl's Family Pizza and Pool Hall. Make that *Pearl's* Family Pizza and Pool Hall, Jacob corrected himself when he noticed that the *P* had blanked out in the blue neon sign in the front window.

The aromatic scent of baking pizza dough and spicy herbs assaulted them when they stepped through the front door. The sound of Italian accordion music blasted from every corner speaker.

Pearl's was packed. Nearly every red-and-white-checked table was full. There was a line for takeout, a line for eat-in and a line for drinks. Servers shouted orders and filled beer and soda pitchers, the phones were ringing, and two men behind a glass counter flipped circles of pizza dough high up in the air, then caught it again.

"You go ahead and order," Clair said over the din. "I'll get us a table."

Several minutes later, Jacob joined Clair at a table beside the Family Fun Center, a room filled with video games and pinball machines. He nearly spilled the icy mug of beer and soda he carried when two young boys burst out of the room and exploded past him.

"Hoodlums," he muttered. He handed Clair her soda and a paper wrapped straw, then set a red plastic number card on the table that read 17.

"They're just little boys." Clair ripped an end off her straw's wrapper, then blew the paper sleeve at Jacob and hit him on the nose. "Don't you like children?"

Frowning, he crinkled the paper into a little ball and threw it back at her. "Sure. I used to be one. I was a hoodlum, too."

"I don't believe you." She took a sip of her soda, then set her elbows on the table and rested her chin on her fisted hands. "Hoodlums don't read Hemmingway or know the square root of twenty-five thousand."

"They might if they had a parole officer who believed in education."

"You were in *jail?*"

The shock in her eyes reminded him how little she knew about life outside her own secluded world. And how little she knew about him.

What would she think of him if she really *did* know him? Jacob wondered. Living in the slums of New Jersey was as far from South Carolina high society as a guy could get. Survival was all that mattered in the neighborhood where he'd grown up. When he'd been a kid, he'd seen things, even done some things, that would make Clair's skin crawl.

Hell, it made *his* skin crawl.

"Juvenile hall, actually." He could still remember the sound of the metal bars they'd slammed closed behind him. Could still feel the panic of being locked inside a cage. "I was fourteen."

"You were only a child."

"Where I grew up, fourteen is definitely not a child." He watched the two boys who'd nearly bumped into him run to a table across the restaurant where a man and woman were sharing a pizza. The quest for quarters, he thought with a smile. "And the man whose car I stole didn't much care how old I was."

"You made a mistake." Clair pressed her lips firmly together and lifted her chin. "You said yourself that your mother had abandoned you and your brother, and that your father was an alcoholic. Surely the judge took that into account."

"Sure, he did." Jacob stretched his long legs out under the table. "He sent my brother to a foster home, and me to a Newark boys' home."

"He separated you and your brother?" Indignation squared her shoulders. "That's terrible!"

"Turned out to be the best thing that could have happened." Evan had only been eleven at the time. Jacob remembered how hard those first few weeks had been for both of them. "It gave Evan a stable home with a decent family for four years and me a goal."

"What goal?"

"Not to end up like the rest of the kids I was hanging with, and definitely not to end up like my father. After I finished high school, I went to work for a bail bondsman and discovered I had a knack for finding people who didn't want to be found. Two years later I got my private investigator's license, then opened an office in Jersey."

"What about your brother?"

"He finished high school, then got a four-year scholarship to University of Texas." Jacob stared at the condensation on the mug in his hands. "Neither one of us has looked back."

Is that why Jacob had set no roots? Clair wondered. Why he'd chosen a job that kept him moving? Because if he was still for even a moment, he might look back and be reminded of what he'd left behind? Or of what he'd never had?

Strange, she thought. She couldn't remember her past, and he couldn't forget his.

"And Evan," she asked, "where is he now?"

"He owns a construction company about twenty miles outside of Fort Worth, a small town called Kettle Creek." Jacob shook his head. "A masters in science and he ends up swinging a hammer. Go figure."

There was pride in Jacob's voice, not criticism, Clair noted. "Why didn't you go to college, too?"

"Degrees are for nine-to-five people who like ladders and schmoozing with the boss.'' He crossed one boot over the other. ''My life is simple. No time clock to punch, no yard to mow, no quarts of milk to pick up for the little woman on my way home from work.''

Clair wasn't certain how the conversation had moved from getting an education to yard work, then to marriage, nor was she certain whether Jacob was trying to convince her or himself that he had no intentions of ever settling down.

She knew this was his way of letting her know he wouldn't be sticking around after he got her to Wolf River. His job would be over, mission accomplished. As hard as it was for her to hear it, she at least appreciated his honesty. There'd been far too many lies in her life.

More than anything, she needed the truth right now. She needed to know what happened twenty-three years ago. And most especially, *why*.

She knew the answers to her questions were waiting for her in Wolf River. That there were people waiting to give her those answers.

And she knew it was time to go there.

The call for order number 17 interrupted Dean Martin singing ''That's Amore'' and while Jacob went to get their order, Clair sat back and watched the families enjoying a night out. A blue-eyed baby girl two tables over rubbed spaghetti sauce into her blond curls while her older brother picked the cheese off his pizza, then—despite his mother's warning— crammed a huge bite of crust into his mouth. In the far corner, an extremely loud Little League baseball team was clearly celebrating a victory and at another table beside them, a little redheaded girl was having a birthday party with balloons and paper hats. A big pink candle on the cake in the center of the table declared that she was eight.

When she was a child, Clair's birthday parties had either been at the Van Sheever Yacht Club, the Four Seasons Hotel or Emily Bridge Rose Gardens. Never a pizza parlor. Josephine Beauchamp would have been appalled at the very thought.

Clair glanced around the restaurant again, felt an ache settle in her chest. Desperately she wanted to be a part of this. She wanted children and birthday parties and Little League games. A minivan or SUV. A white picket fence. Rosebushes. A dog.

And—she watched Jacob come toward her, holding the pizza high as he dodged children running underfoot—she wanted a man who would bring home a quart of milk on his way home from work.

They ate pizza, played video games and Skee-Ball, and that night, as the rain pounded the roof and thunder shook the motel walls, they made love with the same intensity as the storm overhead, both of them knowing their time together was growing shorter by the hour. By the minute. By the second…

Ten

"Welcome to Wolf River, Miss Beauchamp." Grinning broadly, Henry Barnes enclosed Clair's hand between both of his own. "You have no idea what a pleasure it is to finally meet you."

The silver-haired man, dressed in jeans, a white button-up shirt and cowboy boots, looked more like a rancher than a lawyer, Clair thought. His handsome face was tan, his years evident in the deep lines at the corners of his dark brown eyes and the brackets alongside his smile. The warmth in that smile took the edge off the icy fear in her blood and the tight knot in her stomach.

For the last twenty minutes, since she and Jacob had driven past the Welcome To Wolf River County sign, then parked in front of Beddingham, Barnes and Stephens Law Offices, Clair had not been able to put a coherent thought, let alone a sentence, together.

Gratefully years of etiquette now took over. "Thank you, Mr. Barnes. The pleasure is all mine."

"Just call me Henry. And you—" he released her hand and turned to Jacob "—are Mr. Carver, I presume. I'm not sure whether to label you a magician or a miracle worker, but as spokesperson for the Blackhawk family, I thank you for bringing Elizabeth—" Henry shook his head "—Clair, that is, safely to us."

Obviously uncomfortable with the compliment, Jacob shifted awkwardly, then accepted Henry's hand. "Jacob."

"I'll get us some coffee." Henry gestured toward two chairs opposite his large oak desk. "Make yourself comfortable and I'll be right back."

"I can wait outside." Jacob turned to Clair after Henry left the room. "This is private and I'm sure—"

"Would you stay?" She touched his arm. "I'm not sure I can do this alone."

I need you, she almost said, and would have meant it in every way. But that, she figured, was the last thing Jacob needed to hear. She would not cling, nor would she beg. It would only embarrass them both.

Hands folded in her lap and shoulders straight, Clair sat in the chair Henry had offered while Jacob studied a miniature train setup in the corner of the office. The detail in the old-time railroad display, right down to the shiny brass bell on the engine and an entire 1800s coal mining town was amazing. She watched Jacob glance at the switch that would turn the train on, couldn't help but smile when she saw the brief glimpse of childlike anticipation in his eyes before he shoved his hands into the back pockets of his jeans.

They'd both been unusually quiet since they'd left the town of Lucky early this morning. She'd asked for no side trips today, not even to take pictures. They'd driven seven hours straight on the Interstate, had stopped briefly for gas and fast food in Lampasas, a small Texas town known for its mineral springs, then were back on the road again.

She understood that the drive today—what might very well be their last day together—was a transition time for both of them. Though she had no idea *how* her life was about to change, she knew without a doubt it would.

And Jacob's would not.

"Here we go." Henry came back into the room carrying a tray loaded with three mugs of steaming coffee and a plate of cookies. "Judy, my secretary, has the afternoon off for a PTA bake sale. We need books for a new library at the elementary school." He set the tray on his desk. "I made my donation early and lucked out with a dozen of Angie Smith's chocolate chip cookies."

"Angie Smith?" Clair glanced up sharply. "You mean Angela Smith, married to Boyd?"

Lifting a brow, Henry sat in a brown leather chair behind his desk. "You know Angie and Boyd?"

"No. I—she—" Suddenly she couldn't speak. She felt as if her life had turned into a connect the dots puzzle and with each new line drawn, she was closer to a completed picture.

"We met her cousin Dorothy in Lucky, Louisiana," Jacob answered for Clair. "She told us to say hello if we saw them."

Henry smiled warmly at Clair. "I'm sure you'll have a chance to do that, especially since Lucas's wife, Julianna, is best friends with Angie's daughter, Maggie."

Lucas, Julianna, Maggie. Clair knew she'd have to ask again later, but she was too dazed right now. Clasping her hands tightly together, she swallowed and leaned forward. "My family," she said quietly. "I need to know what happened."

With a nod, the lawyer leaned back. "We only sent the barest information for Jacob to give to you. Your brothers decided they would rather you heard the details in person, as they already have."

Your brothers.

Clair's heart started to pound furiously. A lifetime of learned patience flew out the window at the lawyer's words. "Please, Mr. Barnes—Henry."

"Twenty-five years ago," Henry began, "on September 23, you were born Elizabeth Marie Blackhawk to Jonathan and Norah Blackhawk. You had two brothers, Rand Zacharius, age nine, and Seth Ezekiel, age seven. Your parents owned a small horse ranch outside of town."

Henry pulled a document from a file sitting on his desk and handed it to her. Clair's hand shook as she stared at the birth certificate. She'd been born at 3:47 p.m., weighed seven pounds, three ounces. Twenty-two inches long, eyes blue.

"We always celebrated my birthday on August 29," she whispered, realizing the birth certificate she'd used her entire life was a phony. "I thought I'd been born in France."

"I already sent you a copy of the newspaper article about the accident." Henry slipped the original out of the folder. ''Your parents' car went over a canyon ravine in a lightning storm and they were killed instantly.''

''But the article said we were all killed.'' Clair looked at the article, but couldn't bear to touch it. ''How is that possible?''

''The conspiracy was an elaborate one.'' Henry's expression was somber. ''It was so unthinkable, no one suspected a thing.''

''A conspiracy?'' She shook her head. ''I don't understand.''

''The night of the accident, the first person to arrive on the scene was Spencer Radick, the sheriff of Wolf River. At first, Radick believed your entire family had been killed in the accident, so he called your father's brother, William. William arrived a few minutes later with his housekeeper, Rosemary Owens, and they discovered that you and your brothers were not only alive, but had suffered very few injuries.''

Spencer Radick, William, Rosemary Owens. Clair struggled to keep the names straight, knew that each one was another number to help her connect the dots. ''My uncle,'' she whispered. ''He took us home?''

''I'm afraid not,'' Henry said sadly. ''William was an angry, disturbed man. He'd been estranged from both his brothers since they married outside their own race.''

Clair furrowed her brow in confusion. ''But then what did he—''

The realization slammed into her like a two-by-four in the chest. She gripped the wooden arms of the chair she sat in, then said raggedly, ''He *sold* us.''

''In a way,'' Henry said, ''though he saw no money himself. He split you all up that night, sent Rand with

Rosemary, Seth with the sheriff, and you with Leon Waters—a crooked lawyer from Granite Springs—a man who specialized in illegal adoptions. You were all adopted out, Rand and Seth each told their entire family had died in the crash. You were too little to understand what had happened.''

"But the newspaper article." Clair looked at Jacob, saw the rigid set of his jaw, then glanced back at Henry. "The death certificates, children missing. Why wouldn't *someone,* a neighbor or another family member, have questioned or discovered the truth?''

"Your uncle Thomas and his wife were already dead. Their son, Lucas, was only a teenager. William's wife, Mary, was a weak woman. It was easier for her to pretend she didn't know what had happened. And their son, Dillon, was just a child himself.'' Henry sighed. "Your uncle William was thorough and he had the money to pay off all the right people. Spencer Radick left town two months later and was never seen again, Rosemary Owens moved to Vermont shortly after that. Leon Waters closed his practice and disappeared.''

"Waters blackmailed my parents a few years ago.'' Clair remembered her mother and father talking about the lawyer. "They paid him to keep my adoption secret.''

"Waters is the scum of the earth.'' Disgust filled Henry's voice. "But if it helps you, the Beauchamps didn't know the truth when they adopted you. You were the perfect child, the right coloring and hair, healthy and young enough that you would forget your past.''

"They lied to me.'' She closed her eyes against the growing ache in her chest. "Let me believe I was their daughter by birth. My mother even told a story about being in labor with me and how nervous my father was.''

''Sometimes the line between the truth and fiction becomes blurry,'' Henry said gently. ''What we're doing here now is making that line distinct and clear.''

''Twenty-three years,'' Clair whispered, then glanced up sharply at the lawyer. ''But how, after all this time, did the truth finally come out?''

''Rebecca Owens, Rosemary's daughter, found a journal after her mother died several months ago. I have copies of that journal in a file for you.'' Henry slid a thick manila folder across the top of his desk. ''Rosemary had written in detail everything that happened that night, plus the names of everyone involved. Most likely it was to protect herself in case William ever came after her and threatened her. Rebecca contacted Lucas, your cousin, who hired me to track you all down. Rand and Seth were easy. You were not. If not for Mr. Carver here, I'm not sure we would have ever found you. We all owe him a debt of gratitude.''

''Yes.'' Clair looked at Jacob, met his dark, somber gaze. ''We do.''

He'd saved her from a marriage she hadn't truly wanted, given her the courage to make decisions for herself, to simply be herself. The past few days had been the most important, most special, most exciting of her life.

When he left, he'd take much more than her gratitude, she thought. He'd take her heart, as well.

She turned away from him, couldn't think about him now, about his leaving. If she did, she was certain she'd fall apart completely. She'd come too far to allow herself to break down here.

Later, she told herself. After he was gone. Only then, would she allow herself to give in to the pain of losing him.

She forced her attention back on Henry and the reason she'd made this journey. The picture was beginning to take shape. Clair understood *what* had happened and *how*.

But there was one more question, possibly the most important.

"Why?" she asked quietly. "Why would anyone do such a horrible, cruel thing to three small children? We were family. Flesh and blood."

"For the same reason most men commit crimes." Henry opened the file and pulled out a thick, stapled document. "Your grandfather's original will. The one that left a very large estate to all three of his sons. Unfortunately, because William got hold of it before anyone else even knew it existed, he created a different, fraudulent will. One that left everything to him alone."

Clair was used to large amounts of money, had an extremely healthy trust fund of her own. Still, as she glanced through the papers, the size of the estate was very impressive.

It appeared that she was about to become five million dollars richer than she already was.

Her hand shook as she handed the will back to Henry. She didn't care about the money. She'd learned only too well that there were some things no amount of money could buy.

"William—" Just saying his name made her stomach feel sick. "Will he go to jail?"

"If he were alive, he would," Henry said. "He died two years ago in a small plane crash. His son, Dillon, left Wolf River when he was seventeen and no one has heard from him since. Your brothers are still discussing whether we should look for him. I believe they were waiting for you to help make that final decision."

Your brothers.

The last two dots to make the picture complete.

To make it whole.

She swallowed hard, drew in a slow breath. "When can I meet them?"

Henry sat back in his chair and grinned. "How 'bout now?"

"Now?" Surely he didn't mean *now,* as in right this minute. Breath held, she glanced at Jacob. He leaned toward her, covered her hand with his.

"They're waiting outside," Jacob said quietly.

"Here?" She glanced sharply at the door, felt her heart knock against her ribs. "They've been here all this time?"

"We all thought it best we didn't tell you until after you heard everything." He squeezed her hand and smiled. "You might have found it distracting."

Distracting? Good Lord, that was putting it mildly. Her stomach rolled, and it suddenly felt as if ice were pumping through her blood. She opened her mouth to speak, but couldn't force the words out.

Jacob looked at Henry. "Give us a couple of minutes, will you?"

"Take your time," Henry said kindly, then stood and left the room.

When the walls around her started to spin, Clair closed her eyes. "I—I'm not ready."

"Come here." He tugged her onto his lap, enclosed her in the warm comfort of his strong arms. "No one's rushing you."

"I'm scared," she whispered. She felt completely foolish, like a child, but she couldn't stop the shaking that had taken hold of her.

"It's all right." He pressed his lips to her temple. "Let yourself go with it."

She curled into him, felt the heat of his body warm her. Beat by beat her heart slowed and her stomach settled. He smoothed his hands over her stiff back, rocked her gently.

Muscle by muscle, she relaxed, melted into him while he tenderly, patiently held her close. The room no longer spun, it held steady and even. Secure. She thought she could sit here with his like this forever.

But there were no forevers with Jacob, she knew. What he offered was temporary. It hurt, but she could accept that.

She would have to accept that.

She eased away from him, touched his cheek with her hand, then smiled. "Thank you."

Drawing in a slow, deep breath, she stood, was thankful that the floor felt steady under her feet. "I'm ready."

When he moved toward the door, her pulse picked up, with anticipation this time, not panic.

Smoothing the front of her blouse with her damp palms, she stared, breath held, as Jacob reached for the knob.

The two men standing on the other side straightened as the door swung open.

Their eyes met.

She couldn't speak, wouldn't have known what to

say if she could. They were so *tall.* Dark hair like hers, the same dark blue eyes. They certainly looked like brothers.

They looked like *her* brothers.

Her neck began to tingle, almost as if someone were lightly touching her with their fingertips. *Strange,* she thought as both men rubbed at their necks.

Shoulder-to-shoulder, they stepped awkwardly into the room, seemed to fill it with their presence. Not knowing what to do with her hands, she folded them primly in front of her, swallowed back the thickness in her throat while she searched for something to say.

For what felt like a lifetime, they all stood there, silently staring at each other.

And then they smiled.

And she smiled back.

It was just that easy.

"Lizzie." The man on the left side held out his hand to her. Rand, she thought. She was *certain* it was Rand.

Tears streaming, she flew across the room and dived into both men's arms. They felt so familiar. They even *smelled* familiar. It didn't matter that she didn't know her brothers, that she couldn't remember them on a conscious level. She *felt* them in her heart, in her soul.

"You're Rand." Not even trying to hold back her tears, she kissed his cheek, then moved to Seth and kissed him, too. "And Seth."

Both of her brothers' eyes sparkled with moisture. She hugged them again, then eased back, struggling to find her voice. "It's so amazing, so wonderful."

"We were hoping you'd feel that way." Grinning,

Rand looked at Seth, then they both grabbed her again and squeezed.

The wonder of it, the magic, had them all laughing. They held on to each other, absorbing the moment and each other. She had no idea how long they all stood there. They felt solid against her. They felt *right*.

They formed a circle of three. The power of that circle coursed through her blood and pounded in her temples.

They finally eased back from each other, though still they did not break contact. "We weren't certain you'd come," Rand said, gazing down at her.

"I had to," she said softly. "But you know that."

"Yeah." Rand nodded. "I think I do."

Stepping back from Rand and Seth, Clair opened her mouth to introduce Jacob, then closed it again.

He wasn't in the doorway.

She glanced over her brothers' broad shoulders and looked into the outer office. He wasn't there, either.

He wouldn't have left without saying goodbye, she was certain of that. But he hadn't wanted to stay and be a part of her family reunion, either. One more way he was letting go, she realized.

Strange how her heart could feel so full, yet so empty at the same time.

"So, little sis." Seth took her hand. "You ready to catch up on twenty-three years?"

Turning back to her brothers, she smiled through her tears. "Yes," she said with a nod. "I am."

Down the street from Beddingham, Barnes and Stephens Law Offices, Jacob sat at a small corner table in the lounge of the Four Winds Hotel. The room was crowded with locals getting off work and—according to a welcome sign outside the lounge—an East Texas Cattle Rancher's convention. A sea of cowboy hats bobbed across the room like boats on Hudson Bay.

He drained the last of the beer he'd been nursing for the past two hours and did his best to concentrate on a baseball play-off game on the television over the glossy oak bar. He thought it was the seventh inning, but he hadn't a clue what the score was. In spite of the fact he was a die-hard baseball fan, he didn't much give a damn, either.

A cocktail waitress named Michelle came over after dropping off a load of drinks at the next table. The blonde picked up his empty glass, then set another beer in front of him and a fresh bowl of peanuts.

"On the house," she said, curving her lips. "I figure if it takes you as long to drink this one as it did the last, it'll be about the same time I'm getting off work."

"Thanks." He managed to work up a smile, knew that there was something seriously wrong with him when he couldn't even find it in him to banter with a pretty woman in a very short skirt. "I'm waiting for someone."

"Two hours is a long wait." Michelle rolled one shoulder in a disappointed shrug. "Let me know if she's a no-show."

"I'll do that." He lifted his glass to her, took in her long legs as she turned and walked away. And felt nothing.

Damn. Something was *definitely* wrong with him.

And that something was Clair.

He'd checked her into a suite at the Four Winds after leaving the lawyer's office. He'd figured after several days on the road sleeping on lumpy mattresses in backwater motels, she'd be ready for plush towels, soft pillows and room service again. He'd left a message for her with Henry telling her where he'd be, then had her suitcases taken up to her room by a bell cap. Jacob was smart enough to know that if he'd gone up to the room himself, the temptation to stay would be too great.

He stared at the white foam head on the beer in his hand, but all he could see was the image of Clair in Rand and Seth's arms, the joy and happiness on all their faces as they'd embraced.

In the past two hours, he'd asked himself where he fit into that scene—if he *could* fit in. And the answer kept coming back.

Nowhere.

What did he have to offer her? He'd made some healthy investments over the years, he didn't even have to work if he chose not to. Still, her bank account made his look like pocket change.

She had a loving family, *two* loving families now. Jacob realized he hadn't seen his brother in a year.

Or was it longer?

Hell, he couldn't keep track, he thought with disgust. He couldn't even remember the last time he'd seen his own apartment. Three months maybe? Like money, time had never meant a great deal to him.

He caught sight of her as she stepped into the lounge, and his heart jumped.

Dammit. No woman had ever made his heart jump like that before.

She made her way through the crowd and sat in the chair opposite his, then made everything worse by smiling. He had to take a drink of beer to wash away the sudden dust in his throat.

"I take it everything went well?" he asked when she just sat there and kept grinning.

"It was wonderful." She leaned across the table, her voice slightly breathless. "They're wonderful. We talked for two hours straight and barely touched the surface. Rand trains horses and he's remodeling our parents' ranch and Seth is, or was anyway, an undercover police officer in Albuquerque. They're both engaged, can you believe it?"

He listened while she told him how Rand had met his fiancée, and they'd rescued wild horses in a canyon, how Seth had met Hannah after crashing his motorcycle in her front yard.

Her face glowed; her eyes sparkled. He thought she looked more beautiful at that moment than any other.

"My cousin Lucas has invited us for dinner at his house tonight," she said, her blue eyes wide with excitement. "He's married and has three-year-old twins, a girl and a boy, and a brand-new baby boy named Thomas. Oh, and he owns this hotel we're sitting in, isn't that amazing!"

"Clair—"

"Oh, and Hannah, Seth's fiancée—" she couldn't sit still in her seat "—she has five-year-old twin girls, too. They're all going to be there. I don't know how I'll keep everyone's names straight." She tilted her head sideways and glanced at his wristwatch. "I need to go up and shower. We're supposed to be there in an hour."

"I can't go."

The smile on her lips froze. "You can't go?"

"I have a meeting in Dallas early tomorrow morning. I'll need to hit the road in a few minutes."

"Oh. Well." She stared at him for a long moment. "Okay."

Okay? He told himself it was good that she wasn't making this difficult, but still…a simple "okay" wasn't exactly what he'd expected.

Hell, what *had* he been expecting? That she'd cry or complain?

Maybe even ask him to stay?

No. That *isn't* what he wanted. Obviously it wasn't what she wanted, either.

He had no reason to feel guilty that he was leaving so quickly, he told himself. None at all.

"Clair." Though he knew it would probably be a mistake to touch her, he took her hand. Her fingers were warm in his, her skin smooth and soft. "I'm sorry I can't hang around for a couple of days, but—"

"Don't be sorry, Jacob." She squeezed his hand. "Please. These past few days have been wonderful. More than I could have ever hoped for. I realize you have your own life and you need to get back to it."

Dammit, it was one thing to make this easy, and another that she was practically holding the door for him.

He let go of her hand and pulled the hotel key card out of his shirt pocket. "I got you a room," he said, heard the annoyance in his voice and felt even more annoyed. "Your suitcase is already up there."

"Thank you." She stood, leaned down and touched her lips to his cheek. "For finding me. For bringing me here. For everything. It's been quite an adventure."

She turned and walked away, her shoulders straight and her chin level. Jacob frowned, wondered what the hell had just happened. His frown deepened as he watched several male heads turn her way as she passed through the throng of people.

And then she was gone.

It's been quite an adventure.

It sure as hell had.

He stared for a long time at the corner she'd disappeared around, then picked up the beer and practically downed it in one gulp.

The waitress appeared a moment later. "You want another?" she asked.

He didn't even look at the woman, just shook his head, then left.

Eleven

With a glass of icy lemonade in her hand, Clair stepped onto the patio of Lucas Blackhawk's house and soaked in the activity surrounding her. Children playing kickball on a thick, green lawn; Rand and Seth arguing over the outcome of a recent baseball game; Lucas standing guard over steaks sizzling on an open barbecue.

So familiar, yet so strange, she thought, watching Lucas studiously brush marinade on the meat with one hand while he fanned billowing smoke with the other.

"The resemblance between them is remarkable, isn't it?" Julianna, Lucas's wife, came out of the house carrying a bowl of macaroni salad. The stunning blonde hardly looked as if she'd had a baby only four weeks ago. "I nearly kissed Seth earlier when he came up behind me in the kitchen to sneak one of the cookies I'd just taken out of the oven.''

"Now *that* would have been interesting," Hannah, Seth's fiancée, said from the doorway. Her baby blue eyes sparkled as she stepped out of the house and set a basket of potato chips on the patio table. Tucking a loose strand of golden hair behind her ear, she gave a wicked grin. "But I have to admit, I almost pinched Rand on the behind a little while ago when he was searching for a beer in the refrigerator."

"I'd have paid good money to see his reaction to that." With a toss of her shoulder-length auburn hair, Grace, Rand's fiancée, joined them on the patio.

"I'm sure he'd be thoroughly appalled," Hannah reassured Grace.

The women all looked at each other and laughed.

Smiling, Clair glanced at her brothers and her cousin. The resemblance *was* remarkable. The distinct, angular features that declared the Native American heritage in their blood, their thick, shiny black hair and tall, muscular build. Even their gestures were similar, Clair thought, watching the men all turn their heads and frown with concern when one of the little girls—Lucas's daughter, Nicole—began to shriek at her brother, Nathan, for pulling her tennis shoe off. The crisis was quickly over when Maddie and Missy, Hannah's twin girls, snatched their shoes off, as well, and soon all the children were barefoot and laughing again.

All except for little Thomas. The sound of the baby's fussing came over the monitor sitting on a patio chair.

"May I?" Hannah asked Julianna. "I know I

hogged him all afternoon, but it's been so long since I've held a baby.''

"Be my guest." Julianna swept a hand toward the open door. "Though I suspect you'll be holding one of your own before long."

"Oh, I hope so." Hannah's eyes softened at the thought. "I decided if our bed and breakfast doesn't succeed, we'll just fill all those bedrooms with children."

"I've tasted your baking." Julianna slipped an arm through Hannah's and together they walked into the house. "Trust me, you'll succeed."

Clair felt an ache in her chest as she stared after the two women. They had everything she'd ever wanted: children, a home of their own, a man who loved them. Clair knew that she was now part of their happiness, part of all their lives, and for that she would be eternally grateful.

Yet still her heart ached.

How foolish she'd been to let herself hope, to dream, to believe that she'd finally met the man—the one man—who might share those hopes and dreams with her. She still didn't know how she'd ever managed to walk out of that hotel lounge without her knees crumbling, or without running back to him and begging him to stay, even just one more day. One more night.

She wouldn't have changed one thing that had happened between her and Jacob, unless it could be for him to want her, to love her, as deeply as she loved him. And no amount of wishing in the world could make that happen.

"Clair?"

Realizing that Grace had been talking to her, Clair

did her best to cover that she hadn't been listening. "I'm so sorry," she said, felt the heat of her blush on her cheeks. "You were saying?"

"Just how excited we all are to have you here." Grace tilted her head and studied her soon-to-be sister-in-law. "Is something wrong?"

"Of course not." Even as her eyes started to fill, she forced a smile. "Nothing's wrong."

"Baloney." Frowning, Grace took the glass from Clair's hand and set it on the patio table, then took her hand and led her inside the house. "Time for girl talk."

"I'm fine," Clair protested, but couldn't stop the tear that slid down her cheek. *Damn you, Jacob Carver.*

Grace took Clair to the den, then tugged her down on the leather sofa beside her. "Something's bothering you, Clair. Tell me what's wrong."

"Nothing. Really." How pathetic she must look, Clair thought miserably and struggled to hold on to her last thread of composure. "It's just that…so much has happened. I'm feeling a little emotional, that's all."

"How incredibly insensitive we've all been." Her lips pressed into a thin line, Grace shook her head. "So you *are* in love with him, then."

Shocked, Clair simply stared. Grace couldn't know. No one could know. It wasn't possible.

"All this talk about weddings and babies," Grace went on. "After what you've been through. I'm so sorry."

"You—I—" Completely frazzled, Clair didn't know what to say. "Please don't be sorry."

"We could invite him here," Grace said firmly.

"Maybe if he met all of us, and we could explain face-to-face, he would understand why you did what you did."

What I did? What had she done? And invite Jacob here? Clair thought. Good Lord, no!

"Grace," Clair said carefully. "I—I don't understand."

Grace took Clair's hands in her own. "Oliver."

"Oliver?" Clair frowned. "What about Oliver?"

"We know about the wedding," Grace said gently. "How you left the church."

Clair blinked. Grace was talking about *Oliver?*

In spite of the situation, in spite of the ache in her heart, Clair started to laugh. Startled, Grace stared in confusion.

"What's so funny?" A smile on her lips, Julianna came into the den and looked at Clair, then Grace.

"I have no idea." Grace shook her head in bewilderment.

Holding little Thomas, Hannah moved into the room. "Is Clair all right?" she asked, biting her lip.

"I'm not in love with Oliver," Clair managed to say between a mixture of tears and laughter. "I'm in love with Jacob."

Grace lifted a brow; Julianna and Hannah looked at each other, then back at Clair.

"Oh," they all said together.

"Julianna." Grace kept her gaze on Clair. "Go tell the men they can feed the kids and we women will be out in a little while. Hannah, let's you and me take Clair upstairs where it's quiet."

"Please don't fuss over me." Clair looked at all the other women. "I'm fine. I don't want to be a bother and—"

"You are no bother," Grace said while Julianna hurried outside and Hannah waited anxiously. "We're family now, Clair. We're here for you. All of us."

Upstairs, they all listened quietly while she poured her heart out, then each one of them hugged her in turn. It didn't seem to matter that she'd only just met these women. It felt as if she'd known them forever.

In the love and comfort they offered, Clair was certain that somehow, one day, her shattered heart would mend.

Family.

That single word made her throat thicken and the tears start all over again, but this time they were tears of joy.

Jacob slammed the nail into the two-by-four, then stood back and gave the window frame a solid shake. The house was a mere skeleton, but it was taking shape quickly; the first story was nearly complete and the sheeting for the roof was ready to drop in place. The sound of skill saws and men hammering from inside the framework mingled with the smell of freshly cut wood and damp concrete. Overhead, white puffy clouds floated on a deep blue sky.

With the hot Texas sun on his back and a hammer in his hand, Jacob moved to the next window frame. Sweat poured freely down his brow and between his shoulder blades, but he didn't mind. It had been a long time since he'd worked with his hands like this, even longer since he'd worked side by side with Evan.

Too long, he thought. Too damn long.

"You gonna stare that nail into the stud, or hit it?"

Jacob swiveled a look at his brother, then turned back to the window frame and drove the nail in with one powerful swing of his arm.

"Not bad for an apprentice." Evan stepped through what would be the back sliding door of the house, one of three custom homes, each on one-acre lots that Carver Construction was under contract to build. He opened the top of a large cooler sitting beside the house and pulled out two bottles of cold water.

"Apprentice, my ass." Jacob took the water Evan offered, then tipped his head back and guzzled half the bottle. "I taught you everything you know."

"You mean you taught me everything *you* know." Evan leaned one well-muscled shoulder against the bare wood of the doorjamb. "Which took all of five minutes."

Jacob shot a look at his brother that would have had most men backing up. Evan simply grinned, then took a long drink from his own bottle.

Evan was a man in his element, Jacob thought. Relaxed, confident, his dark, long hair covered with a thin layer of sawdust. The blue bandanna wrapped around his head gave him the rough, wild appearance of a desperado, a look that Jacob knew was popular with the ladies. Lord knew there'd been a steady stream of "friends," as Evan as called them, traipsing through the work site this past week.

"So when you gonna finally tell me why you've been hanging around here for the past week doing manual labor with those lily-white hands?" Evan wiped at his mouth with the back of his hand. "I figured either the law's after you or it's a woman."

Because Evan was too close to the truth, Jacob turned his back on his brother and slammed another nail into the window frame. "Can't a guy visit his brother without accusations and the third degree? You want me gone, say so."

"Ah, so it *is* a woman." Evan ignored Jacob's attempt to start a fight. "So what's the deal? She start looking at wedding rings and cooing over babies? That would send you running."

"Evan, just shut the hell up." Jacob dropped the hammer into the work belt slung low around his waist, was furious he couldn't stop the twitch tugging at the corner of his eye. "And I'm not running, dammit. It just wouldn't work, that's all."

It *wouldn't,* he'd told himself a thousand times over the past two weeks. How could it? With her background, her money, all the people who loved her and cared about her, worried about her, what was left for him?

"Well, I'll be damned." Evan's jaw had gone slack. "My brother, the Great Jacob Carver, the man who stands as an icon for the rest of the single male gender, has finally fallen."

"The hell I have." He might have pulled off the lie if he hadn't denied it so hotly. "She got under my skin for a few days, but that's behind me."

"Yeah, I can see that," Evan said with a grin. "That's why you haven't gone back to Jersey and you've been busting your butt pounding on nails. Because it's all behind you."

"That does it." Jacob unbuckled his work belt and threw it at a pile of scrap wood. Pieces of two-by-four went flying. "I'm outta here."

He stomped off, got maybe ten feet, then whirled around and stomped back. "She went to *Cotillion,* for God's sake!"

Still standing calmly against the doorjamb, Evan frowned in confusion. "She went to where?"

"Never mind." Jacob dragged a hand through his hair and shook his head. "It just wouldn't work."

"I believe you already said that." Evan pushed away from the doorjamb, then stepped back from the house and called up to his foreman. "Hank, pack it in. Full day's pay for the crew and first round of beer at The Bunker on me."

The men scrambled at their boss's generous offer. Within minutes, the site was cleared, leaving Jacob and Evan alone.

"So." Evan folded his arms and faced his brother. "You gonna tell me, or do I have to beat it out of you?"

"As if you could," Jacob said irritably, then sighed. He nodded at the cooler. "Got any beer in there?"

With a grin, Evan opened the lid again, dug through the ice to the bottom, then pulled out two cans and tossed one to Jacob.

Jacob popped the top and stared at the foam rushing out. "It's complicated."

Evan shrugged. "Since when did you ever do anything that wasn't? Why don't you just tell me her name."

"God, even *that's* complicated." He blew out a breath, then decided he might as well start at the beginning.

"Twenty-three years ago…"

Pappa Pete's sat on the corner of Main and Sixth. The '50s diner had been there since…well, since the '50s. It was glass and chrome, white Formica counters and red vinyl booths. The food was good, the prices fair and the service terrific.

"You gonna finish those?"

Clair polished off the last bite of hamburger she'd ordered, then glanced up at Seth. His expression was hopeful as he stared at the French fries still on her plate.

"Yes, I am," she said evenly. "And don't think I didn't notice there were some missing after I returned from the ladies' room."

"That was Rand." Seth looked at his brother, whose handsome, rugged face suddenly turned innocent.

"Not me." Rand held his hands up, then looked past Clair's shoulder and lifted his chin. "Hey, do you know that woman over there? She's trying to get your attention."

"What woman?" Clair turned to look, but didn't see anyone. "I don't see—"

The fries had been cleaned off her plate when she turned back. Folding her arms, she sat back in her seat and frowned at her brothers. "That was rude and unforgivable."

"One chocolate shake with extra whip cream, just like you boys ordered for the little lady." Madge, the middle-aged platinum-blond owner of Pappa Pete's, set the shake down in front of Clair.

"Forgive us now?" Rand asked, lifting one brow.

Clair smiled and reached for a spoon. "Absolutely."

The past week had flown by. There'd been two meetings with the lawyer to finalize the paperwork for the estate, a bridal shower for Grace and Hannah and a christening for baby Thomas. Her head was still spinning from all the activity, but she'd been thankful for the distractions.

Anything to keep her mind off Jacob.

It had helped to share her heartbreak with Julianna, Grace and Hannah, but Clair knew that she had a long, long way to go before the pain of losing him eased. And in spite of everything, in spite of the emptiness in her soul, she still cherished every minute they'd shared and grieved for what might have been.

"I say we go find him and kick his butt."

Startled, Clair looked up at Rand's words. His eyes were narrowed in anger, his gaze locked on Seth. *Darn it.* Her brothers knew exactly where her mind had drifted, and the person she'd been thinking about.

"No argument from me," Seth replied tightly.

Clair had been careful not to let her feelings show this past week. Though Rand and Seth had no details, they were well aware of the fact that their sister had fallen in love with Jacob.

"I'm fine," Clair insisted and squared her shoulders. "I appreciate your concern, but really, I'm fine."

Rand shook his head. "She said she was fine twice in the same sentence."

Seth nodded. "Doesn't sound fine to me."

It hardly seemed possible that in such a few short days these two men could come to mean so much to her. Twenty-three years had slipped away and they were family again. Yesterday the three of them had gone to the ravine off Cold Springs Road where their parents had lost their lives, and where their own lives had been torn apart. They'd held hands there, stood as one, and felt the peace fill them, felt the broken bond heal and grow strong in the love surrounding them.

Their parents' had been there, as well, watching them, smiling. Clair had felt their presence, knew that they were happy now, that they could finally be at rest.

When her eyes started to tear, the heat in Rand and Seth's eyes cooled.

"Dammit," Seth muttered. "He made her cry. Now I really am gonna go find that jerk and kick his butt."

"I'm not crying over Jacob," she said, shaking her head. He was part of her tumultuous emotions, Clair thought, but only a part. "I'm crying be-cause...because I love you both so much."

Though they'd shown each other how they felt over the past week, she was the first one to say the words out loud. It threw Rand and Seth a curve ball.

They were silent for a long moment, then Seth said, "So can I have your shake, then?"

"Touch it—" Clair pulled her glass closer "—and you'll see whose butt gets kicked."

They all grinned at each other, then Rand cleared his throat and reached across the table to take her hand. "I love you, too, Liz."

Rand and Seth both had been careful to call her Clair all week, but every so often, the name they'd always known her by—Lizzie—would sneak out. Every time it happened, she'd feel a little catch in her throat and a hitch in her chest.

"Me, too," Seth added, then hugged her.

It felt so good, she thought.

Almost whole.

She'd booked a flight out tomorrow morning for

Charleston, was anxious to see her mother and father and begin to rebuild their relationship. Though they'd talked on the phone every day, Clair hadn't told her adopted parents yet that she would be moving to Wolf River. She thought she should do that in person, knew that they were not going to easily accept her leaving South Carolina.

"Sorry, boys, but I've got to get back to the hotel." She slipped out of the booth and gave both Rand and Seth a peck on the cheek. "Grace and Hannah are meeting me there so I can try on a bridesmaid dress."

"Someone getting married?" Rand asked.

Clair rolled her eyes. In one week, Rand and Seth were having a small double ceremony in the same church where their parents had been married. Clair was flying back to Wolf River the day before the wedding, and if all went well with her parents this week, she intended to ask them to come with her.

"Adagio's at eight tonight," she reminded Rand and Seth of the reservations she'd made at the hotel restaurant. "My treat."

The day was pleasant, warm with a soft breeze and the scent of fall lingering in the air. Scarecrows and cornstalks decorated the windows of the local merchants and banners announced a Halloween Festival in three weeks. Julianna was in charge of the dime toss booth and Clair had already been recruited to help.

She couldn't wait.

It was a short walk to the hotel and Clair strolled casually down Main street. People passing by smiled and waved. Sylvia, a waitress from Pappa Pete's honked as she drove by in a blue pickup. Everyone in Wolf River knew who she was, knew how she and her brothers had been adopted out and were now all back together. There had even been an article in the local newspaper detailing what had happened. The town had welcomed them all with open arms, offered sympathy and support.

In the few short days she'd been here, Clair knew this was where she belonged.

If she couldn't have Jacob, couldn't be a part of his life, or him a part of hers, then she'd make a life of her own. It certainly was time, she thought. It was *past* time.

She started to pass the drugstore across the street from the hotel when she remembered the roll of film she'd dropped off earlier in the week. When she'd first pulled the plastic cylinder out of her suitcase, she hadn't wanted to see the pictures. She'd even tossed it in the trash can, determined to put the past week behind her and move on.

But in the end, her heart won the argument with her head and she'd retrieved the roll of film from the trash, then taken it to be developed, cursing her weakness the entire time.

Just one look, she told herself as she ducked into the drugstore and quickly paid for the developing, then she'd throw every picture away and move on with her life.

She *would.*

Five minutes later, sitting on the sofa in the living room of her motel room, her hands shaking, she opened the package.

The first few pictures were the ones she'd shot on the road—the barns, the fields, the abandoned tractor. The memories of every moment came rushing back and made her smile.

Her heart skipped as she stared at the picture Jacob had taken of her in the shower—just her startled face, thank goodness, then came the pictures she'd taken of him. Remembering that moment made her laugh out loud, but it blurred her vision, as well.

There was a shot of Jacob sitting in his car, frowning at her—she certainly didn't need a picture to remember *that* look. A picture she'd taken of Dorothy, the motel clerk who had told them to say hello to her cousin Angie in Wolf River. Two more pictures of Jacob she'd snapped when they'd stopped along the road, both of them candid.

She was nearly to the end of the roll when she realized there were other snapshots on the roll that Jacob must have taken. They were slightly dark, obviously taken at nighttime. A man and woman coming out of a motel room. She looked closer, then gasped.

Oliver and Susan?

Her gaze darted to the date and time in the corner. The picture had been taken the night before the wedding!

Oliver and Susan?

Jaw slack, she quickly went through the rest of the pictures. Oliver and Susan kissing outside the motel room, another one with the two of them embracing and Oliver groping Susan's bottom. There were three other shots, all showing her fiancé and best friend being extremely intimate with each other.

Good God, what an idiot she'd been!

She was torn between wanting to laugh at the absurdity of it, her outrage at betrayal by two people she'd trusted, and her ultimate relief that she hadn't gone through with the wedding.

Her eyes narrowed slowly.

Jacob had known.

With something between an oath and a groan, Clair tossed the pictures on the sofa. Fisting her hands, she stood and began to pace, muttering to herself as she strode back and forth across the living room of her hotel suite. Jacob had been fully aware of the guilt and shame she'd felt at running out on her wedding the way she had. She'd felt as if she'd let everyone who loved and trusted her down.

He'd known how miserable she'd been, and still he hadn't told her!

Well, she had a few things to say to Mr. Jacob Carver. She'd track him down like the dog he was and then she'd tell him he could go straight to—

The knock on her door had her whirling. Grace and Hannah were going to get an earful about his, Clair thought as she threw the door open.

"Wait until you—"

Her mind went blank when it was Jacob standing there, not her future sisters-in-law.

He lifted a brow. "Until I what?"

"*You.*"

Jeez. Jacob had imagined several different scenarios of how Clair would react when she saw him— anger, joy, even a cool calm—but *this,* this wild fury caught him completely off guard.

"Clair, is something—"

She started to slam the door, but he managed to get his boot in the way before it could close. She'd already turned on her heels and stomped across the living room to the sofa. She picked up a handful of pictures, stomped back toward him and threw them at him. They fluttered to the ground.

"What in the world is wrong with—"

He caught a glimpse of one of the photos that had landed faceup.

"Oh."

Dammit, dammit. He'd completely forgotten about the pictures he'd taken of Oliver and the blond bimbo. He never would have given her that roll of film if he had.

No wonder Clair was so hot.

Crossing her arms, she faced him, her lips pressed into a thin line. "Why didn't you tell me?"

So much for the carefully thought out speech he'd prepared driving here. In the blink of an eye, he and Clair were running in a different direction than the one he'd planned.

And why did that not surprise him?

Closing the door behind him, he squared off with her. "Because after you ran out of that church, you had enough to deal with," he said simply.

She lifted her chin and pointed it at him. "You knew, had *pictures* of my fiancé having an affair, and you kept it from me."

"I just told you, I didn't think—"

"You certainly didn't think, buster." She jabbed a finger at his chest. "You let me wallow in my guilt, worry that I'd left poor Oliver standing at the altar, when all along he was sleeping with Susan—my best friend, for God's sake!"

"And if I had told you that the jerk was cheating on you," he said irritably, "do you really think you would have felt better? You'd just found out that your parents had been lying to you your entire life. Did you really need to know that the man you nearly married and your so-called 'best friend' were lying, as well?"

"It isn't a question of whether I'd feel better or not. It's about the truth. I needed the *truth*." She flounced away from him, throwing her arms out in frustration, then suddenly she turned back, her eyes wide. "Oliver knew you knew, didn't he? That's why he called your motel room before he called mine. He wanted to talk to you before me, so he could find out if you'd told me."

"I have no idea why he called." Lord, she was beautiful all riled up like this, Jacob thought. Her cheeks were flushed, her eyes flashed blue sparks. "You spoke to him, remember? Not me."

"I'll just bet he offered you money not to tell me, didn't he?" She moved close, the expression on her face daring him to lie. "How much?"

He was getting angry now, the last thing he'd come here to do. But she wanted the truth, so he'd give it to her. "Twenty-five thousand dollars."

She went still at the figure, then her mouth dropped open. "Twenty...five...thousand?"

"And another twenty thousand to bring you back to Charleston."

Because her knees were too weak to hold her, Clair stumbled backward to the sofa, then sat. It felt as if all the blood had drained from her face, and with it, some of her fury. She was simply too stunned to be angry.

"You didn't take it," she whispered. She knew he hadn't, could see it in his eyes, could *feel* it in her heart. "Why?"

"He tried to buy you back," Jacob said tightly. "Like you were a car or a goddamned watch. He put a price tag on you, and that just ticked me off."

She stared at him for a long moment, then carefully

asked, "Is that why you came back?" she asked. "To tell me about Oliver?"

"No." He moved in front of her, reached for her arms and pulled her up from the sofa. "I spent the past week with my brother in Kettle Creek, working on one of the houses he's building there."

"You said you had an appointment in Dallas. That's why you—"

He laid a finger on her lips. "I did have an appointment. A referral from Henry. But I turned the job down and somehow just ended up at my brother's. He's swamped with work and I hung around to give him a hand."

She was glad he'd gone to see his brother. She really was. Maybe they'd talk about his visit later. But right now it was not the most important, the most crucial subject on her mind.

"You didn't answer my question, Jacob." She refused to let herself hope, refused to throw herself in his arms and beg him to stay. But her voice wavered as she asked, "Why did you come back?"

"For you, Clair. I came back for you."

Her heart started to pound fiercely. "Why?"

His thumbs lightly brushed her collarbone. "With every yard of cement I poured, every nail I drove in, I thought about you, here in Wolf River, with your family."

Thrilled by his words, but still cautious, she searched his face. "What about my family?"

"I realized that while you were trying to find your past, I was running away from mine." His dark gaze held hers. "And that I was running away from what I wanted the most, which was you."

When she opened her mouth to speak, he shook his head.

"I couldn't see any way around our differences. Money, social standing, family." Lightly he traced his knuckles along her jaw. "You deserved so much more than I thought I could offer. Then I—"

"Jacob—"

"Don't you know it's rude to interrupt, Miss Beauchamp?" he said with a frown. "Now be quiet."

She pressed her lips firmly together, thought she might burst if he didn't hurry and get out whatever it was he was trying to say.

"Then I stood back and looked at the house I was pounding nails into. There was a lot of finish work to do—walls, roof, plaster—but it had a solid foundation and a strong framework." He cupped her chin in his hand. "I figure if I can't give you all those other things you deserve, I can at least give you that. A solid foundation and framework. If you'll have me, we'll work together on the rest."

If she'd have him? The flutter of hope she'd felt a moment ago took full flight. "You—you want me?"

He smiled, then brushed his lips against hers. "I don't just want you. I need you. I need you beside me when we go to bed at night, in the morning when we wake up. I need the sound of your laugh and the enthusiasm in your eyes when you experience something new. I love you, Clair. I want to marry you. I want babies and a house with a white picket fence, Little League games and piano recitals. God help me, we'll even do that cotillion thing if you want."

Her knees turned to water and Clair was certain if he hadn't been holding her, she would have sank to the floor. "You love me?" she whispered. "You want to *marry* me?"

"I love you," he repeated. "I think I've been in love with you since the moment you turned toward me in that church and asked me for a ride."

He loved her. Wanted to marry her. The joy of it swelled in her chest and tightened her throat. When she said nothing, just stared at him, she saw the panic settle in his dark eyes.

"I know I was a fool to let my pride get in my way," he said urgently. "But now I'm asking, I'm begging, please marry me. God, Clair tell me you love me, too."

Laughing, she threw her arms around his neck, then kissed him. She felt the relief shudder through him as he circled his strong arms around her and kissed her back. "I do love you," she gasped, dragging her mouth from his. "And yes. Yes, I'll marry you."

"Thank God," he muttered, closing his eyes. "I was afraid I'd lost you."

"You didn't lose me, Jacob," she whispered against his mouth. "You found me, remember?"

Lifting his head, he grinned down at her. "I guess I did. So, can I keep you?"

She smiled back at him through her tears. "I'm yours, Jacob. I always have been. I always will be."

He kissed her again, a deep, soulful kiss. A kiss filled with promise. With truth.

They were both breathing hard when he finally pulled away and looked down at her. "I don't care where we live," he said raggedly. "I'll build you a house, a big house. We'll fill it with babies and a couple of dogs and a hamster or a fish. My brother wants to bring me in as a partner, expand his business outside of where he is now. I could set up an office anywhere.''

''Jacob.'' He'd be the first person she'd tell, she decided. The first person to know what she planned to do. ''I want to live here, in Wolf River,'' she said, her voice shaking. ''I'm going to buy The Four Winds.''

''The hotel?''

''I know that Lucas has wanted to sell it for a long time, but he's been looking for the right buyer. *I'm* the right buyer.'' Her smile widened. ''I know I'll have a lot to learn and I'll have to work hard, but I can do it, Jacob. I know I can.''

''No doubt about it, sweetheart.'' He slid his hands down her back and tugged her close against him. ''No doubt at all.''

The thrill of his touch, the joy of the kisses he trailed along her jaw, overflowed her heart. To love that one special man, to be loved back, it was everything she'd ever imagined. She took his face in her face and looked up at him.

''I have to fly back to South Carolina tomorrow and see my parents,'' she said softly. ''Will you come to?''

''I have a better idea.'' He pressed his lips into her palm and gazed back at her. Her smile widened.

And together they said it.

''Let's drive.''

*   *   *   *   *

If you enjoyed what you just read,
then we've got an offer you can't resist!

Take 2 bestselling
love stories FREE!

Plus get a FREE surprise gift!

Clip this page and mail it to Silhouette Reader Service™

IN U.S.A.	IN CANADA
3010 Walden Ave.	P.O. Box 609
P.O. Box 1867	Fort Erie, Ontario
Buffalo, N.Y. 14240-1867	L2A 5X3

YES! Please send me 2 free Silhouette Desire® novels and my free surprise gift. After receiving them, if I don't wish to receive anymore, I can return the shipping statement marked cancel. If I don't cancel, I will receive 6 brand-new novels every month, before they're available in stores! In the U.S.A., bill me at the bargain price of $3.57 plus 25¢ shipping and handling per book and applicable sales tax, if any*. In Canada, bill me at the bargain price of $4.24 plus 25¢ shipping and handling per book and applicable taxes**. That's the complete price and a savings of at least 10% off the cover prices—what a great deal! I understand that accepting the 2 free books and gift places me under no obligation ever to buy any books. I can always return a shipment and cancel at any time. Even if I never buy another book from Silhouette, the 2 free books and gift are mine to keep forever.

225 SDN DNUP
326 SDN DNUQ

Name	(PLEASE PRINT)	
Address	Apt.#	
City	State/Prov.	Zip/Postal Code

COMING NEXT MONTH

SDCNM0203